ST STANISLAUS E S LIBRARY

000
Looking for home
Richardson, Arleta.
PB Ric

P9-DJL-016

Ethan to the ground. Clutching tightly, he surveyed his new home while the stationmaster lifted Alice and the little boys from the wagon. Fields stretched as far as he could see around the building, but large trees shaded the yard. It seemed a long way from the road to the broad steps that led to the door.

The sun was disappearing behind the roof, and Ethan felt his heart sink with it. He mustn't let the others know, of course. They depended on him. So once again, he straightened his shoulders and tried to look in charge.

"Take Simon's hand, Alice, and I'll hold Will. Thank you, sir. We'll be fine now."

PBK
Ric

Richardson, Arleta

Looking for Home

DISCARDED

Cathedral Grade School
352 Center Street
Winona, MN

DEMCO

LOOKING FOR HOME

by Arleta Richardson

DISCARDED

Cathedral Grade School
352 Center Street
Winona, MN

Chariot Books™
David C. Cook Publishing Co.

Chariot Books™ is an imprint of Chariot Family Publishing
Cook Communications, Colorado Springs, CO 80918
Cook Communications, Paris, Ontario
Kingsway Communications, Eastbourne, England

LOOKING FOR HOME
©1993 by Arleta Richardson for text and Patrick Soper for illustrations

All rights reserved. Except for brief excerpts for review purposes, no part of this
book may be reproduced or used in any form without written permission from the
publisher.
Cover design by Helen Lannis, interior design by Mark Novelli
First Printing, 1993
Printed in the United States of America
97 96 95   6 5 4

Library of Congress Cataloging-in-Publication Data
Richardson, Arleta.
          Looking for home/ by Arleta Richardson
                  p. cm.–(The Orphans' journey; bk. 1)
          Summary: In 1907, while starting a new life in a Christian orphanage,
eight-year-old Ethan and his three younger siblings hear about the prospect of
being sent west on an Orphan Train and pray to stay together.
          ISBN 0-7814-0921-7
          [1. Orphans–Fiction. 2. Orphan trains–Fiction. 3. Christian life–Fiction.]
I. Title. II. Series: Richardson, Arleta. Orphans' journey; bk. 1.
PZ7.R3942Lo 1993
[Fic]–dc20

                                                              92-46259
                                                                   CIP
                                                                    AC

Contents

To John and Jennie
With God's help they made a success
of all that life handed them.

Introduction

In about 1850 New York, New Jersey, Pennsylvania, and other states on the east coast were troubled by the number of uncared for and abandoned children in their large cities. Orphanages, county poor farms, and foundling homes were filled to capacity. To the annoyance of some and the distress of others, many homeless children lived on the streets, stealing to stay fed and running afoul of the law. Counties were unable to provide for children when parents had died or could not care for them.

In New York, Charles Loring Brace, founder of the Children's Aid Society, began a new system of welfare for orphans and dependent children. His idea was a simple one: send these abandoned children from the big cities to the western states and distribute them to rural families who agreed to take them into their homes.

The children were gathered into groups and placed in railway cars for the trip west. These cars, designated "Orphan Trains," were life-changing instruments for the thousands of children who rode on them from approximately 1854 to 1929, when the system was abolished. The children were put on display in small towns and villages along the route. Having been notified in advance of their coming, families could look them over and choose the ones they wished to take.

Among those who benefited—or suffered—under those arrangements were four children from a family in Pennsylvania. Ethan, Alice, Simon, and Will Cooper were not their real names, but the children did live, and Briarlane Christian Children's Home was there to care for them.

"Ethan" is now ninety-four years of age and remembers some of the details of his early life with clarity. I have tried to weave his memories into the story and to show how four lives were formed, in part at least, by the circumstances of the days in which they lived.

I greatly appreciate the information and encouragement offered by Ethan's children, all of whom are a wonderful monument to the man that Ethan grew to be.

Arleta Richardson
1992

ETHAN IN CHARGE

Little beads of sweat stood on Ethan's upper lip. He licked the corners of his mouth to wipe them off. It was sure hot for being only May, not long past sunup either. He kept a careful hand on the squirming baby and reached for the flannel that had been his ma's petticoat. It was an awful lot of cloth, but he couldn't see anything else suitable for a diaper. With two big pins he held the bottom of the petticoat in place, and the rest of it he wrapped around several times to cover the top of the baby.

"Doesn't look right to me."

Ethan glanced down at five-year-old Alice, who was kneeling on the floor and watching.

"You should talk. How you going to fasten your stockings to your vest? You put it on backwards."

"Had to. Can't reach the buttons if they're in the back."

"Stand up and turn around," Ethan said. "I'll fasten it

for you. Then I've got to dress the boys. Mrs. Kenny'll be here right soon."

"Are we really going to leave Molly with her, Ethan?" Alice's brown eyes were troubled.

"We don't have a choice. The Home won't take little babies. You heard Russell say that he almost couldn't get Will in."

Ethan was glad that Alice had her back to him. An eight-year-old boy couldn't let his sister see the tears that came no matter how hard he swallowed.

"Now, put your dress on and brush your hair. I'll braid it when I finish here."

As he scrubbed Simon and Will, Ethan reflected on the days that had led up to this morning. Until a few months ago, his life had been pretty ordinary. The Cooper clan had never known anything but the drafty, run-down house on the desolate edge of nowhere. Didn't everyone have burlap stretched over broken windows, and cracks a boy could stick his hand through? It was home, and they were content.

Ethan was old enough to know that they would not have fared even as well as they had, were it not for Mary and Seth Kenny. Since Pa was away from home more than he was there, the family would have been hungry and cold many times had it not been for their kind neighbors. Before Molly came, Ma used to rock Will in the evening and tell him about the year she and Pa had come to this house.

"That was before any of you were born," Ma said. "The Kennys came and helped us move in." She looked around the room and sighed. "It looked worse than this, I can tell you. But we were glad to have a home before the twins got here. Seems like Pa never got around to fixing things up much."

"Where's Pa?" Simon's voice broke into Ethan's thoughts.

"I told you, Simon. He's gone to work on a boat."

"Is he coming back?"

"Probably not," Ethan replied. "But we don't care. We won't be here."

Simon nodded and submitted to the wet comb going through his hair. Ethan knew that the little boy wouldn't ask about Ma. Simon hadn't mentioned her since the day he had sat under the kitchen table and watched the men carry her out to the cemetery. No one had even thought to look for Simon until late that evening when Rachel discovered him, asleep under the table, and put him to bed.

"He won't remember," she had said. "He's too young."

It seemed that she was right. Simon had awakened the next morning and joined the others at the table as usual. He didn't even look toward the bed where Ma had been lying for so many weeks.

It must be easier to forget when you're only three, Ethan thought.

Ethan hadn't forgotten. He didn't say anything about missing Ma, mostly because no one talked about it. But once in a while, the subject came up.

"Why did Jesus take Ma to heaven, Ethan?" Alice might ask.

Ethan knew the answer, but he paused to consider.

"Ma was tired, Allie. It's hard to get any rest when there are nine kids in the house. Remember she read to us from the Bible where Jesus said, 'Come unto me all ye that labor and are heavy laden, and I will give you rest'? So that's what He did. He gave her rest."

One part of Ethan was glad that Ma wasn't sick any longer, but a bigger part wished that she would come back. He needed help taking care of things. He didn't need it bad enough to wish that Pa would come home, though.

Ethan's eyes wandered over to the lard pail that Pa had used as a lunch bucket. How many times had Ethan been ordered to trudge into town to get that bucket filled with beer for Pa? More times than he wanted to remember. In fact, there wasn't much about Pa that Ethan did want to remember. How disappointed Ethan had been when Pa refused to allow him to go to Sunday school with the Kennys.

"I don't want the church folks thinking they have to give their old clothes to my family," Pa said. "We'll get along on our own."

Well, that was past. Ethan wouldn't be going after Pa's beer again. And he had known for some time that the four older ones in the family wouldn't be able to support everybody for long. He had heard Russell and the others discussing it.

"What can we do, Russ?" Rachel had asked. "Someone has to look after them better than we've been doing. Ethan shouldn't have to take care of Molly. Simon and Will are more than enough for him to watch. He won't get to school at all this winter if we leave it like this."

Russell had nodded and slumped further in his chair.

"I know. With you working out at Higginses', and Walter and Jake and me finding jobs where we can . . ." His voice trailed off, and Ethan thought that Russell suddenly looked almost as old as Pa. Then Russ spoke again.

"I've been thinking on it. I heard about this county asylum over at Briarlane. Mr. Peat's hired man used to live there. They take orphans until they're sixteen. I think we'd better send the little ones. Even if Pa is still living, we're not going to get any help from him."

"You going to send all of 'em?" Walter asked.

"Not the baby. They won't take infants. Just Alice, Simon, Will, and Ethan. Mrs. Kenny says she'll keep Molly."

"I'm big," Ethan had protested. "I can look after myself when you're gone. And I'll go to school every day. Do I have to leave?"

Rachel gathered him up and hugged him. "You're only eight, honey. You need someone to cook for you and take care of your clothes. Besides, the little boys need you. What would they do in a strange home with no big brother? They're too young to understand not being with family."

Reluctantly Ethan had agreed that this was so and resigned himself to getting ready to leave the only home he had ever known.

Now the morning of departure had come. There certainly wasn't much to get ready. Rachel had gathered the

few garments they would not be wearing, and the
belongings of all four children hardly made a bulge in the
flour sack in which she had packed them.

Besides the clothes, each of them had a personal
treasure. Alice was taking the rag doll that Ma had made
for her. Simon had a whistle offered by Jake as a going-away
gift. Will would not be parted from his "pony"—a cherry
wood branch to which someone in the distant past had
nailed a leather strap. As for Ethan, his treasure was known
only to himself. It was an old watch case he had found in
the field, and it held a picture of Ma.

Will was hollering, and Ethan realized that the little
boy's ear had been scrubbed enough. Quickly the long black
stockings, short pants, and cotton shirt were pulled on,
then Ethan plopped Will on the bed beside the baby. The
sun was higher, and he would have to hurry and get himself
ready to leave. Mrs. Kenny would arrive any minute to walk
into town with them and meet the streetcar that would
take them to the county seat. From there they were on
their own.

Mrs. Kenny appeared as Ethan finished combing his
own hair. She was cheerful as she wrapped Molly in her
shawl and grasped Alice by the hand.

"Have your trolley money, do you?" she asked.

Ethan dug into his pocket and pulled out the three
nickels Russ had given him for the fare.

"Rachel says it won't cost anything for Will if I hold
him. He's only been two for a few months now."

"Humph," Mrs. Kenny snorted. "They aren't losing any

money. All four of you will fit on one seat. But they'll fatten you up at the Home. Hear tell they have a farm and a big garden."

Ethan had decided not to think about Briarlane any sooner than he had to, but Simon was quick to hear the word farm.

"Cows? Will they have cows and horses?"

"Wouldn't be surprised," Mrs. Kenny answered. "Probably pigs and chickens and whatever else they run on those places. You'll have lots to eat, and maybe learn to farm too. Well, are we ready?"

The younger children followed her out the door and Ethan stood for a moment looking around the familiar room. In spite of Rachel's assurance that they would be back home as soon as things were better, he had a feeling that he would not see this house again. A lump formed in his throat, and he shut the door quickly and dashed after the others.

The walk to town would take longer than usual, because Will would have to be carried part of the way. They were not out of sight of the house when Alice stopped in the road.

"Lolly!" she cried.

Mrs. Kenny stopped, too. "What's the matter? What's a lolly?"

"Her doll," Ethan answered. "Wait here. I'll run back and get it."

The little boys flopped on the ground, and Mrs. Kenny leaned against the fence post.

"We'll never make it to town at this rate. Don't know why I didn't think sooner. Ethan, long as you're going back, get my boys' wagon to carry these young ones."

The going was a little faster after that; nevertheless it was almost two hours later when Mrs. Kenny and the children stood in front of the hotel where the streetcar would pick them up. The warm May day had darkened, and heavy clouds promised a shower. If only Rachel and the boys had been there to see them off—but of course they had to work. Ethan straightened his shoulders and tried to look like an elder brother who could take charge. He was responsible now.

THE JOURNEY BEGINS

Ethan watched the rain trickle down the streetcar window and shifted as much as he could without waking Will. In the seat across from him, Alice and Simon were sleeping. Ethan's eyes were heavy, but he dared not close them. He had promised to keep watch over the children, and if he failed, they might be put off the trolley.

The motorman had not been pleased when the conductor lifted the three little ones up the step. He eyed them suspiciously when Ethan held out the three nickels.

"What's this?" he said. "Where's your folks?"

"There's just us," Ethan replied. "I've got money for our fare."

The man surveyed the group. Will clutched his stick horse. Simon stood wide-eyed and silent, and Alice hugged her doll tightly, keeping one hand on Ethan's jacket. For a long minute the motorman looked from one to the other of the children, stopping at Ethan who held the flour sack and Will together under one arm.

"You in charge?" he challenged Ethan.

"Yes, sir."

"Where are you going?"

"To Briarlane."

The man scowled. "Hmm. That's the end of the line. We won't get there for a couple of hours." His eyes went back and forth over the silent little group. "You be sure they don't run around the aisles, or I'll have to put you off. And don't you be blowing that whistle." He jabbed a thumb at Simon's treasure.

"He won't, sir." Ethan hastened to reassure the man. "We'll all be quiet and sit still."

"Well, see that you do. And stay up here at the front where I can keep an eye on you."

The nickels were given up, and Ethan shepherded the little ones to the first vacant seats that faced each other.

"Ethan, can I sit by the window?" Alice whispered anxiously.

Ethan nodded. "You can take turns. When we stop, trade places with Simon. That way you both can see out."

The plan worked well. Since no one dared risk the motorman's wrath, there was no bickering or crying. The swaying of the car, the rumble of the wheels, and the splashing of the rain soon lulled the little ones to sleep. In a very short time Ethan's eyes closed too, and he slept as the trolley rattled through the villages and fields toward the county seat.

A hand shook Ethan's shoulder, and a voice brought him upright in his seat.

"Wake up, boy. This here's the end of the line." The motorman stood in the aisle, looking down at the children. "Someone supposed to meet you young 'uns here?"

It took a moment for Ethan's mind to clear, then he shook his head.

"No, sir. We don't know anybody in this town."

The man stared at him. "Tarnation!" he exploded. "What did you come for, then?" He looked out the window at the driving rain, and then at his watch. "I got to get back on my run, but I can't put you out on the road in this drencher. You'd all drown in five minutes." He looked helplessly at the conductor standing in the doorway. "Now what do we do?"

"Better take 'em into the waiting room, Del. Maybe someone will be along to pick them up. I'll take the little gal if you can grab the boys, and we'll make a run for it."

Before he had time to think it through, Ethan was following the conductor and the motorman through the downpour toward the small station. The flour sack slapped against his legs as he ran, and water splashed into his boots.

In spite of their best efforts, it was four bedraggled and dripping children who stood in the center of a room lined with benches. Ethan looked around cautiously as the men shook the drops from their slickers. There seemed to be only two other people present, a man behind a window and a woman sitting on a bench.

The man at the window spoke. "Who you got there, Del? Did you fish them out of the river?" He chuckled at his own question, but Del apparently failed to see the humor of it.

He glared at the stationmaster as he smacked his wet

hat against the wall. "They'll be fishing you out of the river if you ain't careful," he muttered. "I picked these here kids up at Jefferson, and I don't know where they go."

The stationmaster sauntered around the counter and spoke to Ethan. "Where you going, boy?"

"To the county 'sylum. Is this it?"

"Tarnation!" said the stationmaster. "Orphans! Who sent them out alone this far? And on a day like this?"

"Tweren't their folks, I reckon," the conductor commented. Then he turned to Ethan. "Does anyone at the Home know you're coming?"

Ethan shrugged. "I don't know. Is this the place?"

Simon suddenly found his voice. "Are the cows out in back?"

Before any of the men could answer, the woman spoke up.

"Those children are soaked to the hide. Isn't anyone going to dry them off before they shake to death?"

Indeed the four of them were shivering, and Will's teeth were chattering. The stationmaster led them over to the stove in the corner.

"Stand here and dry off a bit," he instructed. "This isn't the Home, but I suppose someone will have to see that you get there."

The children huddled around the heat, and Ethan listened as the men debated their immediate future.

"I got to get that trolley back on the road," Del insisted. "We can't do anything about them."

"Well, I can't leave here until closing time." The stationmaster scratched his head. "I could show 'em the way, but they can't walk in this. Botheration! Guess they'll have to stay here until I lock up. I can drop 'em off on my way home."

Will pulled on Ethan's jacket. "Hungry," he announced.

"We'll have to wait until we get to the Home," Ethan told him. "Rachel says they have lots of good food there."

At the mention of Rachel, Alice burst into tears, and Will began to wail with her. Simon's lower lip trembled, and Ethan hurried to calm the storm.

"Hey—don't worry. We'll be there pretty soon, and you'll like it. Remember the animals and the garden? If you keep howling like that, we'll get put out in the rain. At least we're warm in here."

"Tarnation," Del muttered as he dug into his pocket. "Here, boy. You can have this nickel back. You didn't take up much space." He pulled a packet out of his slicker. "I don't need no lunch. Too late to eat it now, anyway. Feed the little kids there."

Ethan gratefully accepted the offering, and the Coopers were soon munching on big sandwiches, pickles, and cookies. The woman departed with the trolley, and the stationmaster was left to oversee his unusual customers.

Ethan had no problem keeping an eye on everyone during the long afternoon. They were too awed by the strange circumstances to move around the station, and when they spoke to each other, it was in whispers. As for Ethan, his best imagination could not picture the home and life that lay ahead of them. He waited patiently through that wet afternoon for the station to close and the trip to Briarlane to begin.

The children watched with interest as the wagon covered the distance between the trolley station and the edge of town. Their guide, the stationmaster, pointed out the landmarks with the wagon whip.

"That there's the county seat."

Ethan looked at the three-story brick building in wonderment. It didn't look like a seat to him, but this man must know.

"Here's your schoolhouse. You been to school yet?"

"Yes, sir. But Alice hasn't. She can write her name and say her letters, though," he hastened to add. "Ma taught her."

On the outskirts of Briarlane, the wagon stopped in the road that ran past another large brick building. An arched sign over the entrance proclaimed that this was Briarlane Christian Children's Home.

"Is this the 'sylum?"

"Yep."

Ethan slid off the seat and dropped to the ground. Clutching the flour sack tightly, he surveyed his new home while the stationmaster lifted Alice and the little boys from the wagon. Fields stretched as far as he could see around the building, but large trees shaded the yard. It seemed a long way from the road to the broad steps that led to the door.

The sun was disappearing behind the roof, and Ethan felt his heart sink with it. He mustn't let the others know, of course. They depended on him. So once again, he straightened his shoulders and tried to look in charge.

"Take Simon's hand, Alice, and I'll hold Will. Thank you, sir. We'll be fine now."

THE BRIARS

Most of the residents of Briarlane referred to the county children's home as "that shabby old building at the edge of town."

Shabby was evidently in the eye of the beholder, for Ethan Cooper was sure that they were approaching a palace. The closer they came to the big front door, the slower Ethan walked. Could this really be the place Russell had told them about? Ethan had never seen a building so grand. Surely they would not be able to live here! He grasped Will's hand tighter and pulled the little boy up the steps. Should they open the door and walk in, or did one knock at such a place?

The decision was made for him as Simon stood on tiptoe and grabbed a round handle in the center of the door. A sharp bell rang in response to his pull, and the little boy dropped the handle quickly and ducked behind his brother.

Ethan was frightened, but he held his ground. After all, where could they go now? The children heard the echo of the clanging bell, then voices sounded clearly through the heavy door.

"Who has door duty this week?"

"I do. I'm going."

Running footsteps sounded and the door was jerked open. A girl of about twelve stared with open mouth at the little group arranged before her, unattended by any adult.

"Where'd you come from?" the girl blurted. Her eyes scanned the road for signs of some conveyance. "Who brought you?"

"I did," Ethan replied.

"You never. How old are you?" Blue eyes challenged Ethan.

"I'm eight years old, and I did so!" Ethan was indignant. Maybe they wouldn't let them stay, but he wasn't going to have his word doubted.

"Who is it, Shala?" A soft voice spoke from the hallway.

"I don't know, Mrs. Lehman. There's four of them, and a boy says he brought them."

"Well, bring them in and close the door."

Shala stepped back, allowing the children to come into the warm hallway.

They gazed around in wonder. Straight ahead of them a wide staircase led to the upper floor. They could hear feet running and voices calling to one another. The aroma of fresh bread wafted from the back of the building, and Ethan realized that he was terribly hungry.

His heart pounded as he looked at the lady standing before them. What if there was no room for them? Or worse yet, what if this lady didn't want them? He might get along all right, but what would happen to the others? For the first time that day, Ethan felt real fear.

"You've come by yourselves?" the soft voice asked.

"Yes, ma'am. We came on the trolley, and the man from the station brought us here. Is this the 'sylum?"

"This is the children's home, yes. You are just in time for supper. Shala, take them up to Matron to get ready. We'll talk after you've eaten." She put her hand gently on Ethan's shoulder and smiled at him. "What are your names?"

"I'm Ethan. This is Alice and Simon and Will."

The woman nodded. "I'm Mrs. Lehman. Matron will take care of you. Run along now."

Shala tossed her head and marched down the hallway with her nose in the air. "You can follow me if you want to." Her stiff back proclaimed clearly that these strangers weren't her problem. Being on door duty didn't mean she was responsible for what came through it.

When they returned to the main floor with Matron for supper, the long tables in the dining room seemed crowded with children of all ages. It was a bewildering sight to the newcomers. They shrank back against the door as twenty-six pairs of eyes turned toward them.

The lady with the soft voice came to their rescue. "We have a surprise tonight. Here are four more children come to stay. Bert, will you come and take Ethan to your table? And Betsy, make room for Alice next to you. Simon and

DISCARDED

Will may sit with Matron tonight."

A freckle-faced boy grinned cheerfully and led Ethan to a seat. Alice went with Betsy, and Matron shepherded the two little boys to a table. Everyone became silent, and with her head bowed, the lady spoke again.

"Lord, thank You for this day and for the rain that has blessed the earth. You have given us this food, and we are grateful. Bless the new children who have come to be with us. We welcome them in Your name. Amen."

Large bowls of soup, thick with meat and vegetables, were ladled out. Slices of bread and butter were passed around. And wonder of wonders, every child had a mug of cold milk!

Alice looked furtively around the table, then spoke softly to Betsy. "Can we eat all this, or must we save some for tomorrow?"

"You eat it all. You can have more if you want it. We have lots of food here. We grow our own gardens."

This was hard to believe. The garden at home had never produced a meal like this. Alice ate gratefully.

By the time supper was over, Will had fallen asleep with his head on the table. Matron picked him up.

"You come with us," she said to Simon. "Betsy, take Alice up to the girls' room. Ethan, Mr. Lehman will see you in the office. Bert will take you there."

Ethan watched anxiously as the others were led away, then followed Bert down the long hallway and into the office. Mrs. Lehman sat in a chair, and Mr. Lehman stood at his desk studying the letter that Rachel had put in the flour sack with their clothes.

Ethan waited patiently as Mr. Lehman read aloud.

Dear Sir,

Our Pa has left us, and us older ones can't take care of the
little ones any longer. They are good and won't be
any trouble.

> *Ethan Allen, b. November 17, 1898*
> *Alice Carol, b. July 24, 1901*
> *Simon Peter, b. April 24, 1903*
> *William Andrew, b. June 22, 1904*
>
> *Rachel Cooper*

"This doesn't tell us much," George Lehman said.
"We'll have to try and locate the father. If the past is any
indication, he'll probably arrange it so that he can't be
located."

"I'm thankful that we have room," Mrs. Lehman said.
"We don't usually get them four at a time. It's hard to
believe that child took charge of bringing them here."

She spoke as though Ethan were invisible, and he
listened with growing apprehension. They would be
allowed to stay tonight, but would they be sent away
tomorrow? It had looked like a lot of children around the
tables in the dining room. What if they only had room for
some of them?

No, Ethan decided, if they couldn't all stay, he'd take
everyone back home. How this was to be accomplished, he
didn't know, but his mind was made up. They had already
lost half their family. Nothing was going to separate the rest
of them.

Mr. Lehman smiled at Ethan as he stood in front of the

desk. "Well, young man, I hear that you've brought your brothers and sister here by yourself. That was a long trip to make alone."

"Yes, sir," Ethan answered. "But I can take care of them. They depend on me. I'll see that they behave if you'll let us stay."

"Certainly you may stay," Mr. Lehman assured him, "and you'll have help looking after them. Now you've had a long day. Bert will show you where you'll sleep, and tomorrow we'll get better acquainted."

The long room in which the older boys slept was furnished with a cot and a small cupboard for each child. Ethan was assigned a bed next to Bert, who was delighted to have a new friend his own age.

"I'll show you around tomorrow," Bert promised. "This place is pretty nice when you ain't got no family to stay with."

Ethan fell asleep at once, but several hours later he awoke and looked around the strange room. Six beds on his side held junior boys. On the opposite wall five older boys' beds were lined up. Simon and Will were not in this room. If they should awaken, Ethan thought, they would be frightened. Neither one of them had ever slept alone in a bed in his life.

Carefully Ethan padded across the hallway to the little boys' room. There he found that Simon had crawled into bed with Will. Ethan pulled the covers over both of them. For tonight, they were taken care of.

TROUBLE AHEAD

Mrs. Eugenia Quincy shifted restlessly in her pew and looked around without interest. She did wish that Patterson wouldn't insist on attending this simple little chapel every Sunday. There was a perfectly beautiful church in town that was so much more respectable. The wheezy little pump organ here was highly inferior to the magnificent instrument at St. Jerome's. And the people—well, she wouldn't even think about the people. No one in her social set would dream of worshiping in a place like this.

The subject had come up the previous evening.

"Patterson, I don't understand why we can't attend St. Jerome's services with all our friends."

"I know you don't, Eugenia," Mr. Quincy replied. "That's why I've given up trying to explain it to you."

"Really, you are most annoying, Patterson. You have been offered a position as deacon at St. Jerome's, and you've turned it down to usher in that dreary little Briarlane chapel! Do you really feel that place befits your station in life?"

"Why, yes, my dear. I've attended the chapel since I was a child, and it hasn't hindered my reaching this 'station in life,' as you call it. In fact, I would say that I have been helped tremendously over the years. I owe a great deal to that little church."

"Humph. They owe a great deal to you, if you ask me. They certainly couldn't pay the minister if you didn't contribute. Most of the congregation comes from that orphanage, and everyone knows how much money they have. I would think that serving as president of the board at the Briars would be enough sacrifice for you to make."

Patterson had gone back to his paper, but Eugenia hadn't finished speaking her mind.

"I'm certainly in favor of a little charitable work, but must it be something so . . . so religious?"

"I would hardly call teaching Christian values to children too religious," her husband replied. "It seems highly superior to having them grow up on the streets."

"Of course I have nothing against good moral training for them, Patterson. It is right to be interested in their spiritual welfare, but does it have to take over your whole life?"

A glance at Mr. Quincy's face told Eugenia that she had ventured far enough. It was time to back down.

"Oh, never mind. You just don't understand how I feel. But we won't discuss it any further."

"Thank you, Eugenia. You don't know how relieved I am to hear that."

And so this Sunday morning found Mr. and Mrs. Quincy seated near the front of the chapel as the children and staff from the Home filed into their seats across the aisle. Eugenia watched them listlessly, as she did each week. The boys wore denim pants and white shirts, and the girls were attired in light blue dresses covered with crisp white pinafores. Every child looked like the one beside him. She wondered idly if they had individual names, at least.

Suddenly, Eugenia sat up and clutched her husband's arm. "Patterson, look at that perfectly gorgeous child! The one sitting next to Matron Daly. I haven't seen him before. Does he belong there?"

Mr. Quincy looked toward the group. "That must be one of the new children who came last week," he replied. "George Lehman mentioned that four more had just arrived. All one family, I think."

The congregation rose at that moment to begin the service, and Eugenia could say nothing more. But she could not take her eyes away from the sturdy child. His dark hair lay in waves across his forehead, and his wide gaze took in his new surroundings. When the organ began to play, his attention was riveted on it.

As she watched the little boy throughout the service, Eugenia began to daydream. After twelve years of marriage, she and Patterson had no children. This was of little concern to Eugenia, for her life seemed complete with the social affairs that filled her days. As the wife of Briarlane's foremost judge and mistress of the most elegant house in town, Eugenia's time was consumed with teas, literary club meetings, fund-raising activities, and parties.

Now as she looked at the little boy, it occurred to Eugenia that a child like that could enhance her position in Briarlane. Certainly none of her friends had one like him. Their children tended to be noisy and fussy and ill-mannered. She began to picture herself accompanied about town by a small object of perfection. He would be dressed in the latest fashion in a white suit and little shoes that buttoned up the sides. He would walk quietly beside her and greet her friends politely. She would see that he had the latest books and toys to entertain him. By the time the service had ended, Eugenia Quincy had mentally embarked upon motherhood and was enjoying her new standing in town.

It seemed to take forever to bow to the other parishioners, and Mr. Quincy would stop to visit with all his friends. At last they were seated in their limousine and headed for home.

"Patterson, I must have that little boy!"

Her husband turned a startled gaze in her direction.

"You must have what?"

"The child who has come to the Briars," Eugenia said impatiently. "The one I pointed out to you before the service. I want you to see about getting him immediately."

Patterson Quincy regarded her as though she had taken leave of her senses.

"Eugenia, you can't be serious! You know nothing about that child! We are not acquainted with his background or his family. We don't even know that he is available for adoption. How have you reached this decision when you've only seen him for less than an hour, and that from across the church?"

"I know what I want when I see it," Eugenia replied firmly. "And I want that boy."

Mr. Quincy shook his head in disbelief. Nothing in his past experience had prepared him for this moment.

"I propose that we have a quiet dinner before we continue this discussion," he said. "I need time to digest what I've already heard."

Eugenia knew by the set of his chin that this would be the final word on the matter until he brought it up again, so she settled into her corner of the seat to plan her next move. This might be more difficult than she had envisioned. Patterson could be quite determined when he chose to be.

By the time Eugenia joined her husband on the veranda that afternoon, she was confident that her arguments were sensible and well thought out. She was prepared to answer any objections he might bring forth. She relaxed in her cushioned rocker and bent her head demurely over her embroidery, the picture of patience.

After a lengthy silence Mr. Quincy spoke. "Now, Eugenia, suppose you tell me your reasons for wishing to bring a child into the house at this time?"

It was not the way she had expected the conversation to open. Eugenia had not explored that aspect of the situation. There was no reason: she simply had been taken by the handsome little boy and wanted him for her own. But caution told her that this explanation would not satisfy Patterson. Perhaps, she admitted to herself, she was bored and needed a new interest in life. She probably would not do well to divulge that information, either. What reason would sound logical enough to bring Patterson around to her way of thinking?

"Well?"

"Why, any child has a better chance in life in a home with two parents than in an institution, don't you think? And especially a home that can offer him the advantages that we could afford." Eugenia warmed to her subject and hastened on. "The upper floor could be turned into a nursery and schoolroom. I will find a competent woman to take care of him, and he will be a lot of company for us."

"I wasn't aware that you felt the need for more company, my dear. I have been on the board of the Home for ten years, and you've never expressed an interest in taking one of those children under your care. On the contrary, you have avoided any contact with them whatever. Isn't that so?"

Eugenia felt the color rise in her cheeks. "Well, yes. But they really are quite common children. One can't just pick a child off the streets and . . ." Her voice trailed off as she realized that she was backed into a corner. She was at a loss to explain why this child had taken her fancy or why she felt that she must have him. But Eugenia Quincy was not one to give up without a fight. If this approach did not work, she would try another.

"I believe we had better give the subject more thought," Patterson said. "Before one takes on the responsibility of a child, there must be compelling reasons for doing so."

Eugenia said no more, but she was fully committed to pursuing the matter on her own. Let Patterson do the thinking. She would act.

5

ETHAN LEARNS
THE RULES

"Come on, Ethan. Can't you move any faster?" Bert's freckled face was anxious as he watched Ethan tying his shoes. "I can hear everyone in the dining room. Hurry—you can make your bed later."

The boys raced down the big staircase and slipped into their seats just as Matron bowed her head to pray. It had taken Ethan a few days to realize that no one ate the good food in front of him until someone thanked the Lord for it. He wondered why they told God thank You when they worked so hard to grow it.

"I don't know," Bert said when Ethan mentioned it. "Maybe because God makes it rain. I guess we can't do that."

Bert had undertaken the job of teaching Ethan the fine art of weeding the garden.

"You have to turn the hoe over, Ethan. You can't cut anything with that side. Ain't you never used a hoe before?"

Ethan admitted that he had not. The few things that were grown on the Cooper land were weeded by hand. Neither had he fed animals nor picked fruit. But now he was being introduced to farm life, and he found that he liked it.

The two rows assigned to them looked long. Ethan paused and surveyed them carefully.

"Maybe we can do some now, then finish after we play ball," he suggested.

Bert shook his head. "Nope. That won't work. Mr. Lehman or Otis will check to see what we did. Otis runs the farm, and he knows what everyone is doing. We have to finish our jobs. That's a rule."

Ethan had not lived by that kind of rule before. He did what Pa ordered him to do when he couldn't stay out of Pa's way. Sometimes he was punished whether he obeyed or not. As he chopped the weeds he remembered the stinging blows on his legs from Pa's strap when he didn't hurry back from town fast enough. Ethan hadn't seen anyone strapped here.

A sudden shriek from the direction of the barnyard caused Ethan to drop his hoe and run. "That was Simon!" he yelled.

By the time Ethan reached the fence, Otis had the little boy in his arms. In the pen, the hog was pushing his huge snout against the wire.

Simon sobbed loudly. "He bit me! He bit me!"

"Now he didn't bite you, kid," Otis soothed him. "He thought that you had something in your hand to feed him, and he put his tongue out." Otis set Simon back on the ground. "If I was you, I wouldn't try to give chicken feed to the hog anymore. He probably thought your hand was part of the bargain."

Simon clung to Ethan for a moment, then rubbed his wet face with grimy hands.

"He's too big for you to feed, Simon," Ethan told him. "You stick with the chickens. When you get through, come over where I am, and I'll let you help me weed."

"I never had no brother," Bert said as they went back to work. "Did you always take care of yours?"

"Yep. I'm pretty good at it, too," Ethan boasted. "Ma always had a baby to take care of, so she depended on me. I'll look after them until they grow up, I guess."

For the first time in his life, Ethan was not required to keep a watchful eye on the younger children. The habit was hard to break, however, and Ethan never ate a meal without checking to see that Alice and Will and Simon were in their places.

One morning Matron Daly stopped him as he left the dining room. "Ethan, you didn't make your bed again this morning."

"Oh, I forgot. I meant to go back and do it."

"That happens too often," Matron said sternly. "You can't go out with the others until it's done. Go to your room and take care of the bed, then wait there until I come up to inspect it."

Ethan trudged up the stairs and into the big, empty bedroom. There was no reason why he couldn't just straighten it at night before he got back in it. Ma had never been fussy about making beds.

Slowly he patted the covers in place, then sat down on the end of his cot to wait for Matron. He could hear the boys playing under the window and knew they had chosen sides without him. He sighed loudly and looked around.

Across the room the beds belonging to the older boys were neatly made. Idly his eyes wandered along the straight rows. He had not had anything to do with the big boys except to watch them from afar, but he knew each of them by name. Riley always spoke kindly to him, and his bed was directly across from Ethan's. The next bed belonged to Hugh.

Something on the floor between the beds caught Ethan's eye, and he got up to investigate. It was a picture. He sat down on Riley's bed and looked at it carefully. The face that looked back at him was a beautiful one. Soft hair and smiling eyes made Ethan think a little of Ma, and suddenly he was overcome with homesickness.

Before he could put the picture down, a big kid grabbed the back of his collar.

"Hey, kid! What you doing on my bed?"

Ethan looked into the face of Riley Walter.

"Nothin'," Ethan stuttered, but Riley wasn't listening. His glance had gone to the picture in Ethan's hand, and his face looked angry.

"Where did you get that? Have you been in my cupboard?"

Ethan shook his head. "It was on the floor."

"It didn't get on the floor by itself," Riley said. "I've found my cupboard open before, but I never caught anyone at it." He shook Ethan by the shirt. "Don't you know better than to get into other people's things?"

Ethan nodded wordlessly.

"What else you got that doesn't belong to you?" Riley

demanded. "Stand up here and let me look."

Quickly he examined Ethan's pockets and pulled out the watchcase.

"Where'd you get this from?"

"It's mine. I found it in the field at home," Ethan replied in a small voice.

"Sure you did, kid. You never found no watch in a field."

Riley snapped open the lid and looked at the picture. His face softened, and he said, "Who's this? Your ma?"

Ethan nodded.

"Well, I believe that all right. But I'm not sure you didn't pick up this watch case from someone. Here—you take the picture, and I'll just hold on to the case until I find out who lost it. What else you got in your pockets?" Riley poked his hand into Ethan's other pocket and came up with the nickel that the motorman had returned to Ethan.

"Don't tell me you found this in the field too? How come a kid your age has this much money?" Riley eyed the younger boy carefully. "Maybe I better talk to Mr. Lehman about you. We don't go for this kind of stuff around here."

Ethan's face got white and his lip quivered. What if Mr. Lehman sent him away?

"I didn't steal it, honest," he gulped. "But you can have it if you want."

Riley dropped Ethan's arm. "Naw. I won't keep it. But I'm going to check around. You better not have stolen it, or you're in big trouble. Now after this, you stay out of my cupboard—hear?"

Ethan nodded again, and Riley disappeared down the

stairway after tucking the treasures into his overalls. Sadly Ethan pushed Ma's picture into the far corner of his cupboard and sat down to wait for Matron. Riley would never trust him again, and he hadn't even done anything wrong. It wasn't fair. Riley had probably pulled the picture out himself and just didn't notice it. But it wouldn't do to tell anyone about it, Ethan knew. He would just have to keep out of Riley's way.

Matron Daly entered the room and nodded her approval as she checked the bed. "That's more like it. The Lord is pleased with us when we do our work well."

"You mean the Lord cares how I made my bed?" Ethan was doubtful.

"Of course. The Bible says we should do everything as unto the Lord. That means keeping things neat. Come on down to the laundry with me and bring the boys' clothes back up here. Then you can go out and play."

Ethan followed Matron downstairs and waited patiently as she loaded his arms with clean shirts and underwear. As he trudged back up to the big room, he determined that he would not leave his bed unmade in the future. He was wasting valuable time that could be spent outdoors.

As he neared the room, Ethan heard a cupboard door open and shut. He stopped in the hallway and listened. Another click convinced him that someone was in the bedroom. Everyone was supposed to be outside. Who could it be? Ethan peered cautiously through the doorway.

Hugh. Ethan didn't know much about him, but he did know that Hugh was a bully. He often threatened the younger fellows and made them take over some of his chores.

So far Ethan had managed to avoid him. He certainly didn't want Hugh to see him now. Quickly he dropped the clothes on the nearest bed and ran to the stairway.

"What took you so long?" Bert asked when Ethan arrived at the field where the boys were playing. "We need another guy on our side."

As the game went on, Ethan worried about what he had seen. Riley had been right. Someone was going through the cupboards. Should Ethan report Hugh? If the other boy hadn't seen him, he wouldn't know who had told. Maybe Ethan should get advice from Bert.

"Would you tell Matron if you saw someone going through the cupboards?" he asked Bert.

"Like who?"

"Well . . . one of the bigger kids."

"Are you crazy?" Bert stared at Ethan. "You want to get your head broken? You just pretend you don't even see the big guys. It's safer that way."

Ethan pondered the advice as he helped to clear the tables after supper. Maybe it was best to forget the whole thing. He didn't want to be blamed for everything that was missing, though. Maybe he could pray about it. If the Lord was interested in how he made his bed, He might care about this, too. Ethan would remember this when he said his prayers at bedtime.

As Ethan left the dining room, a rough hand pulled him into a corner. Hugh doubled his fist and glared at him.

"You forget what you saw this morning and keep your mouth shut if you know what's good for you," the big boy snarled. "Bad things happen to kids who blab about stuff that don't concern them. You understand?"

Ethan swallowed hard and nodded.

"You better. I can tell Mr. Lehman that I saw you going through our belongings. He'll believe me, 'cause I've been here longer than you have."

Ethan's heart sank. This was the second time today that he had been threatened with someone talking to Mr. Lehman about him. What would happen to the others if he were sent away? Ethan couldn't risk it. He would keep quiet.

"I'm not going to tell, honest."

"It's a good thing," Hugh said. "You know what'll happen if you do."

For several days Ethan had a knot in his stomach. Whenever he saw Hugh glaring at him, he would look away quickly and pretend not to notice.

One afternoon Ethan was sitting on the steps waiting for Bert. Idly he watched Alice as she played dolls with the other little girls.

Hugh came up behind him. "That little redheaded one is your sister, isn't she? I bet you wouldn't want anything to happen to her."

Ethan jumped up and turned on the older boy. His fists were clenched and his eyes blazed.

"If you touch my sister, you . . . you'll be sorry!" he shouted. Then he turned and raced toward the barn, leaving Hugh with his mouth hanging open in surprise.

6

THE PROBLEMS
MULTIPLY

Eugenia Quincy studied her reflection in the hall mirror and pronounced it good. She needed to look her best this morning in order to accomplish the task before her. Satisfied that there was no visible flaw in her appearance, she opened the big front door.

"I'm leaving, Greta," she called to the housekeeper. "I may not be home for lunch, so don't prepare anything."

Stepping carefully into the limousine, Eugenia leaned back against the soft cushions and took a deep breath. If all went according to plan, she would lunch with Patterson and divulge her good news. There was no reason to think that her plan wouldn't succeed. She had never failed yet.

"I want to go out to the Briars, Gridley," she said. "And I'd like you to wait for me."

"Yes, ma'am." Not by a twitch of an eyebrow did the driver indicate surprise at the direction. Surely he was well aware of Mrs. Quincy's aversion to the orphanage, but it was not his place to speculate on the reason for this trip.

As the car purred toward the edge of town, Eugenia reviewed the strategy she had planned. Although she was not well acquainted with the director of the home, Mr. Lehman had always treated her with courtesy and deference. There would surely be no difficulty in persuading him to her point of view. If necessary she could mention that Patterson . . . that Patterson what? She could hardly say that she had come with her husband's blessing, since Patterson knew nothing about her visit, and almost certainly wouldn't have blessed it if he had. Oh, well. Once he had gotten used to the idea, Patterson would go along with her decision.

The big car drew up before the archway, and Gridley opened the door for Eugenia. With something resembling a shudder, she looked up at the sign proclaiming "Briarlane Christian Children's Home," then she walked briskly toward the door. She would much have preferred that Mr. Lehman come to her as her dressmaker did, but she was forced to admit that this was a somewhat different situation.

The door was opened by Bert, who had hall duty this week and was polishing the wood panels as his morning chore. Eugenia glanced at him and drew her skirts around her as she swept into the hallway.

"Please tell Mr. Lehman that Mrs. Quincy desires to see him."

"Yes, ma'am." Bert scurried off, leaving Eugenia

standing by the door. She tapped her foot impatiently. She might at least have been offered a chair while she waited. This was an example of the kind of child that was sheltered here, she thought. Certainly no training in the niceties of life. All the more reason why her errand was an important one.

To Eugenia's gratification, Mr. Lehman himself came out to greet her.

"Mrs. Quincy. What a pleasant surprise. Won't you come in?" He ushered her into the shabby but comfortable office. A fire burned in the grate, dispelling the chill of the early spring morning. A wall of books, a desk piled high with folders and papers, and several chairs completed the scene. George Lehman pulled the most comfortable seat toward the desk for his visitor.

Eugenia looked around the room with barely concealed distaste. Was this where Patterson conducted the board meetings each month? Why in the world had he not done something about the appearance of the place?

Mr. Lehman's voice interrupted her thoughts. "What can I do for you, Mrs. Quincy?"

Eugenia turned her brightest smile in his direction. She might as well dispense with the small talk and proceed directly to the point. The place was depressing, and she had no desire to stay any longer than necessary.

"I understand that you have recently taken in four new children," she said.

Mr. Lehman nodded. "Yes, the Cooper children."

"I want the youngest one."

George Lehman couldn't hide his astonishment. "I beg your pardon?"

Why do men have to be so slow-witted? Eugenia thought irritably. He was acting just like Patterson. What was so hard to understand?

"I . . . we want to adopt the youngest one," she repeated impatiently. "What is his name?"

"William," Mr. Lehman answered automatically, "but—"

"I'll call him Reginald," Eugenia declared. "Can Matron get him ready immediately?"

Mr. Lehman leaned back in his chair and studied his visitor. This was going to be a sticky situation.

"I'm sorry, Mrs. Quincy, but I'm afraid that will be impossible."

"I don't understand."

"The Cooper children are not available for adoption until the father is located," the man explained. "If and when that occurs, they will all go together."

"Together! Ridiculous! Who is going to take four children at one time? Your main concern is placing children in good homes, isn't it? What is the reason for all these silly rules?"

"The Home is under state regulation, Mrs. Quincy. Even if I wanted to separate the Cooper children, I could not do so without the consent of the family."

Eugenia was no longer wearing her brightest smile. She was unaccustomed to being denied anything, and she found the situation most wearisome. As she smoothed her gloves in her lap, her mind tackled the problem. She didn't want to use the last weapon in her arsenal, but there seemed to be no alternative.

"Mr. Quincy has given much to this institution over the years," she said. "I'm afraid I shall have to ask him to withdraw his support unless . . ." Her voice trailed off, but the meaning was clear.

"We appreciate Mr. Quincy's generous gifts," Mr. Lehman said carefully, "but in this instance there is nothing I can do. I'm sorry."

"I expect we'll see about that, won't we?" Eugenia rose and strode haughtily toward the door.

George Lehman hurried to open it for her.

"Good day, Mr. Lehman. You will be hearing from me again."

I'm sure I will, he thought as he watched her leave. The sound of the big front door closing signaled her departure. Watching out the office window, his eyes followed the angry woman as she sailed down the path and entered her limousine. George Lehman felt as though he had done battle with the Furies.

Bert wasted no time in locating Ethan in the barn, where he was sweeping the floor.

"Ya can't guess what I just heard," he whispered hoarsely, "up there by the office."

Visions of both Riley and Hugh approaching Mr. Lehman about him held Ethan speechless. He stared at the freckles standing out on Bert's face and clutched his broom for support.

"A fancy lady in a huge car is going to take Will away. I heard her tell Mr. Lehman."

Ethan had difficulty switching his thinking from the threat he'd been anticipating to a threat unimaginable, and he continued to stare at Bert.

"Didn't ya hear me? I said—"

But Ethan had dropped the broom and grabbed Bert's skinny arm.

"What lady? What car? Did she take Will?"

"Ow! Leggo! I didn't do nothin'! No. She said she'd be back." Bert rubbed his arm and backed off. "I thought you'd want to know."

"She can't do that," Ethan said. "They won't let her take him, will they?"

Bert had regained his composure. "Look, Ethan," he said, "this here is an orphanage. That's the kind of stuff they do—get homes for kids like us. Well, maybe not us," Bert reconsidered, "but little kids like Will, or blond, curly haired girls."

Ethan felt a moment of relief. That would let Alice out. Her hair was red and as straight as it could be. He sank down on a bale of hay.

"She can't have Will. I won't let her. Nobody can unless they take all of us."

Bert sat down beside him. "How you goin' to stop her?" he asked practically.

Ethan's shoulders drooped and he looked at his friend bleakly.

"I don't know. What shall I do?"

Bert chewed thoughtfully on a straw. "Looks to me like this is serious enough to pray about," he offered. "You ever prayed besides 'Now I lay me down to sleep'?"

Ethan shook his head. "Not much. I prayed that Ma would get better, but she didn't. I prayed that Russell would let me stay home, but here I am."

Ethan thought of all that had happened since he'd forgotten to make his bed and Matron had told him that the Lord was interested in how he did his work. It looked like that was all the Lord was interested in. First Riley and then Hugh had threatened him, and now Will was in danger. For someone who hadn't had much practice, it looked like he was collecting a lot of things to pray for. Come to think of it, Ethan told himself, he didn't seem to be very good at praying. Perhaps he'd better begin to make some plans of his own.

"Who is this lady with the car?" he asked Bert.

"She said her name was Mrs. Quincy. I've never seen her before." Bert glanced at his friend. "She said she'd call Will 'Reginald' when she took him home."

Ethan looked disgusted. "Reginald! What kind of name is that? Anyway, Ma named him William, and she can't change that. You've got to help me think of some way to keep her from taking him."

"I don't know," Bert replied doubtfully. "I've noticed that grown-ups do pretty much what they want to when it comes to kids."

This fact had not escaped Ethan's attention. But when it came to the safety of his little brother, he was ready to fight even grown-ups.

"I'll find some place to hide him," he declared.

"Where you going to hide something that big?" Bert wanted to know. "Your cupboard is too small, and they clean under the beds."

"What you planning to hide, kid?" Hugh had appeared out of nowhere.

When neither boy seemed able to answer, he repeated his question.

"N . . . nothing," Ethan stammered. "We—I—didn't take anything."

"So how come you need a place to hide it?"

"He wants to hide—" Bert began, but a sharp poke from Ethan ended the explanation. Hugh looked at the boys sharply, but neither one said any more.

"Won't talk, huh? Well, don't forget that I'll be watching you—and you know what happens to kids who don't mind their own business."

He disappeared out the barn door, and Bert turned to Ethan. "What's the matter with him? What's he mean about minding our own business?"

"I guess he doesn't want us to talk about him," Ethan shrugged.

"I don't want to talk about him," Bert declared. "I don't even want to think about him. We got enough problems of our own."

Ethan nodded agreement. He couldn't tell Bert that Hugh was one of the problems.

7

ETHAN LEARNS TO TRUST

As the days went by and no one appeared to carry Will off, Ethan began to relax his vigil. Probably Bert had misunderstood the conversation he'd overheard. Besides, there were a lot of others things to claim his attention.

One bright spring Tuesday morning Otis made an announcement after breakfast.

"Whitewash day, boys. Bert, Philip, Ethan, and Billy, work on the henhouses. The older fellows come with me."

"What are we going to do?" Ethan asked as he trotted along with the others. "What is whitewash?"

"Paint," Bert explained. "All the outbuildings get cleaned up with it in the spring. I guess it kills the bugs. Makes 'em look better, too."

"The bugs?"

"Naw, silly. Didn't you have a henhouse or pigsty or nothing on your place?"

Ethan recalled the few scrawny chickens that scratched around the Cooper yard. They had roosted in the trees at night. He had to admit that he remembered nothing that was painted.

It didn't take him long to enter wholeheartedly into the process. Paint flew everywhere as the boys happily sloshed big brushes against the wood. An occasional jab at the one working alongside seemed like a good idea, and it wasn't long until boys and buildings had received a generous coat of whitewash.

It was Ethan who noticed the hog snoring peacefully in the dusty pen.

"He could use some cleaning up," Ethan said to Bert. "And you know he has bugs."

Bert looked doubtful. "I don't know if we're supposed to paint hogs. Maybe it isn't good for them."

"It doesn't hurt us," Ethan argued, "and his hide is tougher than ours. Come on. Let's try it."

"You try it," Bert decided. "He might wake up and not like it. Get in the pen, and I'll hand you the paint."

It took only a moment for Ethan to scramble over the fence and into the pigsty.

"I'd stay behind him if I were you," Bert advised. "If he opens his eyes he won't see you first off." He watched anxiously as Ethan approached the big animal with the pail and brush.

"If he starts to get up, come out of there quick," Bert added. "He could knock you down with his snout."

Ethan eyed the hog anxiously. "He does look a lot bigger

in here than he did out there," he admitted. "If he wakes up, I'll get away."

Ethan needn't have worried. The hog was dead to the world and didn't move as Ethan began at his tail and moved up the huge side with the paintbrush. Bert hung on the fence and gazed wide-eyed until Ethan reached the hog's ears. Then there came a snuffle and a snort, and the earth began to tremble.

"Whoa!" Bert shouted. "He's turning over, Ethan. You better move!"

Ethan jumped back, but he wasn't quick enough. Without opening an eye the huge beast flipped to the other side and flattened Ethan to the ground.

"Hey—look at that!" Bert marveled. "He didn't even wake up, and you can paint the other side!"

Ethan wiped the dust off his face and glared at Bert. "Not much, I can't. He's sitting on me."

There was silence while Bert took this in.

"You mean you can't get up out of there?"

"My leg is under him, and I sure can't shove him over again. Now what are we going to do?"

"Won't do any good for me to poke him," Bert decided practically. "I'll run and get Otis. Stay right there."

It's not like I could go anywhere, Ethan thought dismally.*I just hope this hog stays asleep.*

Otis soon arrived with a rake, and after much prodding with the handle, the animal lumbered to his feet and shook his head. Otis scooped Ethan off the ground and ran for the fence.

"I never told you boys to whitewash the inside of the pigsty," he said sternly. "It's a wonder you weren't killed."

"We weren't painting the pigsty, Otis," Bert informed him. "We were painting the hog."

"Painting the hog?" Otis shook his head in disbelief. "If that animal hadn't been so full and so sound asleep, he'd of et you alive. What in tarnation did you want to do that for?"

"Ethan thought it would kill the bugs," Bert explained.

"And he sure had a lot of room to look better," Ethan added. "He's one heavy pig." Ethan rubbed the offended leg and hopped around on it.

"If you hadn't landed in one of those holes he's dug out, he'd 'a busted that leg in two," Otis told him. "Brush as much of the muck off as you can and go on up to the house. I'm sure Matron will be glad to see you."

Otis turned and stomped back to the barn, and Bert translated the message. "He really means she won't be glad to see you. Matron doesn't like messes."

Bert thought for a moment, then his face lit up. "I know! We'll go down to the river, and you can splash around with your clothes on. That'll wash 'em out, and by the time we go up to dinner, you'll be dry. Matron won't have to know what you did."

Suiting the action to the word, the boys raced off to the stream of water running through the farmland. Since they were there, they figured they might as well both enjoy a swim.

"Oww!" Ethan yelled. "This is cold! I think there's still ice in here."

"Keep moving fast," Bert instructed him. "It'll take awhile to get rid of all that dirt and paint."

By the time they emerged, blue with cold and

shivering, a meeting with Matron didn't seem like a bad thing to look forward to.

"I don't care what happens," Ethan declared. "I'm going in to get some other clothes. Come on—let's run."

The boys raced across the field toward the house.

"If we go in through the kitchen and up the back stairs, maybe no one will see us," Bert panted. "The cook will be too busy to notice."

As they neared the back steps, Ethan slowed down and grabbed Bert's arm.

"Oh, no. Look who's on the porch waiting for us."

It was Hugh. The older boy grinned and sauntered toward them.

"What happened to you guys? Fall in the horse trough? I wouldn't go in there if I were you. Matron is in the kitchen." He looked directly at Ethan. "She's looking for you. And so is your little sister."

Ethan forgot about the water dripping from the legs of his overalls and the cold, wet hair plastered to his head. He charged blindly into Hugh with both fists beating furiously. "What did you do to my sister?" he shouted. "Did you hurt her? Where is she?"

Bert grabbed the back of Ethan's shirt and tried to drag him back. "Hey—what are you doing? Cut it out, Ethan!"

Hugh held Ethan at arm's length. "Take it easy, kid. I didn't do nothing to your sister. I just heard her yelling for you. And I heard Matron ask where you were. You'd better go back to the barn until you dry off a little. Whatever she wants you for will be twice as bad if she sees you looking like that."

Hugh's advice came too late. Just at that moment Matron opened the door and stepped out onto the porch. She shook her head as she spied the two soaked boys standing in the yard.

"Oh, my," she said. "Look at you. I hope Will doesn't look that bad." She looked around, and then back at Ethan. "He was with you, wasn't he?"

Ethan backed off and looked at her blankly. Matron hurried down the steps and shook Ethan's shoulder.

"Wasn't Will with you? Where is he?"

"No, ma'am," Bert answered for him. "Nobody was with us. We've been—"

But Matron had turned quickly and reentered the house. Ethan seemed rooted to the spot until Bert pulled at him. "Come on. Let's find Alice. She knows where Will is."

"I think Ethan knows where he is too," Hugh said. "I heard you talking about hiding something. What else would it be if you ain't stole nothing? Guess I better go up and tell Mr. Lehman about it. There's several things I could tell him, you know."

Hugh stuffed his hands in his pockets and turned away.

"No! No!" Ethan ran after him. "You can't tell him! I never took anything, and I didn't hide anything. I don't know where Will is."

Hugh stopped and looked at Bert. "Why don't you run and find Alice?" he suggested. "Tell her that Ethan is back here."

Bert took off, and Hugh brought his attention back to Ethan. "Well, maybe I will go up to his office and maybe I won't. It all depends."

"Depends on what?" Ethan inquired anxiously.

"I could use a little help with something I'm planning," Hugh replied. He rubbed his chin thoughtfully. "I might forget what I heard if you was willing to help me." He continued to look at the younger boy shivering in front of him, then he shook his head. "Naw—I probably wouldn't be able to trust you. After all, I did find you sneaking around the bedroom the other day."

Ethan didn't even consider reminding Hugh that he, not Ethan, had been the one sneaking around. Mr. Lehman must not hear anything that would cause him to send Ethan away. If he had to go, he was determined to take the others with him.

"You can trust me," Ethan insisted. "You can. I'll do anything you say. But I have to find Will first."

Bert and Alice were racing toward them, and Hugh turned away again. "I dunno. I'll have to think about it," he said, and disappeared around the corner of the house.

Alice grabbed Ethan around the waist. "I can't find Will," she sobbed. "He was playing out there on the grass, and then he was gone. I've called and called him. You have to find him, Ethan. You have to!"

"We will," Ethan assured her. "We'll find him in no time. He's too little to go very far. Where did you see him last?"

Before Alice could answer, Matron reappeared.

"Boys, come in this instant and change your clothes. We have enough trouble around here without two cases of pneumonia."

"But, Will," Ethan protested. "I have to find Will."

Matron took both boys by the arm and headed for the

porch. "No buts," she said. "We've got folks looking for him. He's probably fallen asleep out there in the haymow, and he'll be back here before you're dressed. Now get upstairs."

Ethan was in despair. Why did he always have to worry about two things at once? If only he had remembered to make his bed that morning a few weeks ago, this never would have happened. He wouldn't have caught Hugh going through the cupboards, and Hugh wouldn't have anything to tell Mr. Lehman. And why hadn't he kept a better eye on Will? Then, too, what if Otis decided to report that the hog had been painted? How had he gotten himself into so much trouble without even knowing he was doing it?

Bert broke into his dismal thoughts with another idea. "Ethan, what if that lady came back in the big car and got Will?"

Ethan had almost forgotten about her. His face turned white and his eyes widened as he stared at Bert. "No," he shook his head. "She couldn't have. We'd have seen her."

"Not from the river," Bert reminded him. "We weren't in sight of the road the whole time."

"We've got to tell someone you heard her say she was going to take him!" Ethan exclaimed. "We can tell Matron and she'll let Mr. Lehman know."

Bert sat down on the edge of the bed. There was a worried look on his face.

"I don't think we can do that, Ethan. I wasn't supposed to hear that, and Matron doesn't like listening in. We'd be in big trouble with Mr. Lehman."

Ethan sank down on his bed and stared bleakly at his

friend. "Yeah. That's right. We'll have to think of something else."

When Will was nowhere to be found, the rest of the afternoon turned into a frantic search of the grounds around the house. The barn was gone through from top to bottom. The older boys walked through the woods, calling for Will. By supper time everyone was tired and discouraged. The only thing that had been found was the little stick horse with the leather strap. It lay beside the fence where its small owner had dropped it.

Ethan had trouble eating his supper, and it was even harder to fall asleep. If Will were out wandering around, he would be frightened and crying. Even if the lady had taken him, he would be lonely and afraid. Ethan rolled over and buried his face in his pillow so that none of the boys would awaken and hear him crying.

A gentle hand was laid on his shoulder, and Matron's voice spoke softly. "Ethan, I came to tell you that everything will be all right. Mr. Lehman will find him. Shall we pray about it together?"

Ethan nodded. He listened as Matron asked the Lord to protect Will and bring him back safely. Ethan wondered if the Lord was really listening. It seemed to him that his life had gotten a lot more complicated since he found out that God was interested in him. Was Matron really sure that prayers were answered? He figured it might not be a good thing to ask, so he remained silent.

"Ethan, have you heard the story that Jesus told in the Bible about the Good Shepherd?"

"No."

"Do you want me to tell it to you?"

Ethan nodded again, and Matron settled on the edge of his bed. "There was a man who had a hundred sheep, like the ones out here on the farm," she began. "Every morning he would take them out to the pasture to eat, and he would watch them carefully. Every evening he brought them back to their pen. The shepherd would stand by the gate and count them as they went in. When he had counted one hundred, he would lock the gate and go home for his supper.

"One night the shepherd counted only ninety-nine sheep. He looked around closely, for he knew them all very well, and discovered that the very smallest one was missing. Quickly he locked the gate, then went back to look for the lost sheep. He searched for a long time. He didn't give up, even though it was dark and lonely out in the pasture. Finally, after many hours, he found the little one who had wandered away. The shepherd carried him back and put him in the pen with the others. Then he could go home."

Matron paused and looked at Ethan. "Jesus told that story because He wants us to know that He is the Good Shepherd, and we are His sheep. He knows about Will. He knows right where Will is. The Shepherd wants us to trust Him. Do you think you can do that?"

"I'll try," Ethan said. "I like that story. If someone is taking care of Will, I guess I can sleep."

Matron patted his head and left. Ethan, comforted, turned over and slept.

8

EUGENIA QUINCY
MAKES A DECISION

Eugenia Quincy pushed the food around on her plate and pondered her day's activities. She'd returned to the orphanage after giving Mr. Lehman a few days to rethink his position. She had entered the office with a cheerful spirit and a determined step. Mr. Lehman seated her and waited politely for her to open the conversation.

"I hope you have reconsidered your decision about the young Cooper child," she said. "You do know what advantages we have to offer him. Mr. Quincy is in a position to expedite the adoption, and I would like to have it taken care of at once."

"Perhaps I didn't make myself clear when we spoke earlier," George Lehman replied. "This is not a matter within my jurisdiction. Any living parent must be located and must give permission for an adoption to take place. We have not located Mr. Cooper. Also, as I mentioned, the older children in the family do not want the younger ones separated. We will honor their wishes."

Unbelievable! Eugenia thought. *Here is a man who doesn't realize the danger of opposing me. Well, he soon will.* She continued to smile, although her eyes flashed a warning which Mr. Lehman did not fail to note.

"I see," she said. "I'm sure that if you give it careful thought you'll find that there are loopholes in every situation, even this one. In the meantime, there could be no objection to my taking the child for a few days to get him acquainted with his future home, could there? I'd appreciate it if you would ask Matron to get him ready at once. I have errands to complete, and I am running late."

George Lehman was becoming impatient with this woman. In deference to her husband's position, he had to treat her with civility, but he might as well be talking to a tree stump. She obviously hadn't heard a word he'd said.

"I'm sorry, Mrs. Quincy. We appreciate your interest in Will, but the boy is too young to be away from the people he knows. It wouldn't be wise to upset him that way." Mr. Lehman arose. As far as he was concerned, the matter was settled. But as he again watched Eugenia Quincy march toward her car, the uncomfortable knowledge that it most certainly was not settled stayed with him.

Eugenia sighed and put her fork down.

"You aren't eating, my dear. Are you not feeling well?" Patterson's voice broke in on her thoughts.

"I'm fine," she replied. "I'm just restless. There's not much going on since summer has begun. I need something to occupy my time." She glanced furtively at her husband, but he had gone on with his dinner and did not appear to take the hint she had given him.

"I am very busy at this time, or I would arrange for us to get away,'" Mr. Quincy said finally. "I'm afraid I can't spare Gridley right now to go with you either. Why don't you take Clara and run up to the lake for a few days? You could drive the small car. Perhaps I can join you later in the week."

This was not what she'd had in mind, and Patterson knew it. Nevertheless her voice was even as she answered him.

"Thank you, dear. I'll think about that."

As she wandered discontentedly about the house that evening, the suggestion began to seem more attractive. It had been a long time since she'd had to fight this hard for something she wanted. The longer it took, the more determined she was to have it. She needed to get away to think this through.

Her mind made up, Eugenia called Clara to her room. The dark-haired young servant appeared promptly.

"Clara, pack bags for you and me to go to the summerhouse. I'd like to leave early tomorrow morning."

"Yes, mum. Will the mister be going?"

"No, there will be just the two of us. Ask Greta to prepare some food for us to take."

"How much food, mum?"

"Oh, I don't know," Eugenia answered impatiently. "Ready enough for a week at least. Mr. Quincy can bring what we need if I decide to stay longer."

Clara departed and Eugenia threw herself down on the chaise lounge. Was she the only one in this house who could make a decision about anything? At least she was sure of one thing. She would have a foolproof scheme for getting that child before she returned.

The following morning found Eugenia Quincy attired in a long driving coat, her large hat secured firmly with a gauzy scarf, ready to depart. Gridley fastened the bags to the back of the car, settled the big wicker basket beside Clara in the backseat, and stepped back. Eugenia took her place behind the wheel and drew on her gloves.

"Have a safe trip, madam."

Eugenia nodded. "Thank you, Gridley."

The car chugged out the circular drive. The fifteen-mile trip covered roads on which the travelers were likely to meet nothing more than an occasional horse, and the little car did not begin to reach the speed of the limousine.

The route to the lake took Eugenia past the Briars. Though she usually ignored the Home as she passed, this morning she recalled with annoyance her unsatisfactory conversation with George Lehman. She really should report the man to Patterson for his insubordination—but that would mean telling him what she'd been up to. As the car approached the arched sign over the entrance, Eugenia slowed down and regarded it with distaste. Stubborn man!

All at once the car stopped so suddenly that Clara was forced to lunge for the basket before it slid to the floor.

"Oh! What is it, mum?"

There was no answer, but Clara watched in fascination as Eugenia stepped down from the high seat and walked to the fence that surrounded the lawn. There stood a small boy staring with obvious delight at the vehicle in the road.

Eugenia smiled at him. "Hello, there. Do you like that car?"

The boy nodded. "Pretty car!"

Eugenia looked around the yard and toward the building. There was no one in sight.

"Would you like a ride in the pretty car?"

His eyes lit up, and he nodded vigorously.

Quickly Eugenia leaned over the fence and picked him up. Before the dumbfounded Clara could catch her breath, she found the little boy on her lap and the car moving again.

"Oh, mum!" she gasped. "What have you done? You can't just take him! What will the Home say?"

"I know what I'm doing, Clara. Just hold on to him."

"Oh, mum!" Clara wailed. "They'll be after us!"

"Don't be ridiculous, Clara," Eugenia said. "We'll have him back in a few days. There are so many children running around in there that they'll never miss him."

What sounded like a sob from the backseat irritated Eugenia. "For goodness' sake, Clara, stop that sniffling! If you must know, I've already talked to Mr. Lehman about taking the boy."

It seemed unnecessary at this point to add that Mr. Lehman had refused permission. She didn't need a terror-stricken maid on her hands for the rest of the week.

Little Will Cooper shrieked and jumped with delight as

the car gathered speed and the wind rushed through his hair. It took all of Clara's attention to keep him from falling over the side in his excitement.

On the morning after Will's disappearance, Ethan and Bert retreated to the old wagon stored behind the barn. There they sat, bare legs swinging over the tailgate, pondering the best way to proceed with their day. Aside from Matron's chores, they had been assigned no job for the morning. Everyone was concerned about the missing boy, and the most judicious plan seemed to be to keep out of their way. The older fellows had again been dispatched to the fields and the woods to search.

"The only place no one has looked is the house that lady with the big car came from," Bert remarked finally. "They don't know about that."

"Maybe we should do that ourselves," Ethan suggested. "If we found him there, they'd be so glad they'd forget to ask how we knew."

Bert's eyes sparkled. "Hey! That's a great idea! Let's do it!"

The boys jumped from the wagon and took off toward the road.

"Where are we going?" Ethan was breathing hard as he kept up with Bert.

At the question, Bert stopped. "I don't know."

"You mean you don't know where she lives?"

"Nope. All I know is she said her name was Mrs.

Quincy." Bert looked discouraged for a moment, then brightened. "Shala! She'll know. She's been here since she was little, and she knows everything. We'll ask her."

"You ask her," Ethan said. "I'll wait here for you."

He sank to the ground as Bert sped off. Shala had not been overly cordial to him since the day they had arrived. She probably wouldn't give him any information if he did ask her.

Bert soon returned with the good news that Shala had known exactly where the Quincy house was. She had demanded to know why Bert was interested.

"The only reason I could think to tell her was that we wanted to see that big car up close. That would be no lie. I would like to look it over, wouldn't you?"

Ethan nodded, and they hurried on their way to the edge of town. Their steps slowed when they came in sight of the house, surrounded by green lawn and trees. It was an awesome sight. A broad porch encircled the entire structure, and wide steps led to the big doors. Sunlight danced and sparkled from every window, and white paint gleamed in the morning brightness.

"Wow!" Ethan breathed. "That's almost as big as the Briars. I wonder how many kids live here?"

Bert didn't answer. He was busy wondering whether they should approach the front door or go around to the back.

"What are we going to say when she comes to the door?" Ethan asked. "Shall we just ask if we can see Will?"

"We better find out if he's here or not," Bert replied.

"Maybe the one who has door duty today will know."

It seemed a long time after they had pulled the bell before the door opened, revealing a large woman wrapped in a big white apron. She gazed in surprise at the two boys standing before her with dusty bare feet and overalls cut off at the knee.

"Are you Mrs. Quincy?" Ethan blurted.

"Naw!" Bert tugged at his arm. "That ain't Mrs. Quincy. That's the Matron."

"Now that you have that settled, boys," Greta said, "what is it you want?"

"We want to see Mrs. Quincy," Bert answered. "We want to ask her something."

"Well, I'm afraid you can't do that," Greta replied. "Mrs. Quincy left town yesterday, and I don't know when she'll be back."

Ethan's shoulders sagged with disappointment. "Did she take Will with her?"

"Will? Who's Will? Clara's the only one who went along."

"Will's my little brother, ma'am. We can't find him, and we heard—"

A sharp poke from Bert's elbow reminded Ethan that they were not to mention having heard anything.

Greta eyed them sharply for a moment, her forehead wrinkled in puzzlement. "I'm sorry, boys. I can't help you. I don't know anything about your little brother."

She stepped back into the house, and two dejected boys trudged back to the road. What were they going to do now?

MR. QUINCY ENTERS
THE PICTURE

Two unhappy boys sat beside the road to think over their situation. The problem seemed to be bigger than they could handle.

"Matron said that the Good Shepherd knows where Will is," Ethan said. "I wonder why He doesn't tell us?"

"I don't think He talks out loud to people," Bert offered. "In the story, He brought the lost sheep back Himself. So He'll bring Will back, too. We might as well go home and wait for him."

Ethan nodded, but neither boy moved. The sun was warm on their backs, and the breeze carried the smell of new grass and lilacs. After being so sure that they were going to the right place, disappointment seemed to leave them motionless.

"If the lady didn't take Will, who do you suppose did?" Ethan wondered. "Somebody must have. He was too little to go alone."

"I don't know," Bert sighed. "Not a whole lot of people go by our road. Only folks on the way out of town." Bert thought over his own reply and sat up straighter. "We can go look in town and ask people if they saw him," he exclaimed. "Someone just might have noticed a little boy they hadn't seen before."

Ethan was willing to agree with this theory, and they lost no time in heading for the center of the little town. Horses and buggies were lined up along the main street, and people walked back and forth in front of the stores. The excitement of seeing all this activity slowed them down a bit.

"I remember coming past here from the trolley station," Ethan said. "It's better to come this way. You can stop and look in the store windows."

This they did, lingering long over a display of bicycles and toy wagons. They dared not venture inside the stores, since they had no money to spend, but there was much to see from the street.

"Look, Ethan!" Bert grabbed his arm. "There's a lady with a little boy! He looks something like Will!"

The direction Bert pointed was across the road, and the two were moving rapidly away from them. Without looking either way, Ethan started into the dusty street.

Bert grabbed the straps of Ethan's overalls and pulled him back.

"You gotta watch out or you'll get run down," he warned. "Look what's coming."

A large wagon, pulled by a team of horses, lumbered by. Buckets hung from the back, and ladders were strapped on the sides. Something that looked like a huge barrel lay in the bed of the wagon. The boys watched in fascination as it passed them in a cloud of dust.

"That's a fire wagon," Bert informed Ethan. "They can come in a hurry if something is burning."

"Did you ever see them do it?" Ethan asked.

"Well, no. We never had a fire out at the Home. We'd probably see it a lot if we lived in town."

"I think I like where I am better," Ethan decided. "There's more stuff to keep us busy."

Suddenly he remembered what they had started out to do. Looking anxiously down the street, he saw that the woman and little boy had disappeared.

"Come on," Bert said. "If we run, maybe we can catch them."

Several minutes later they slowed down. It was no use. The pair were nowhere in sight. The boys began to walk again.

"I think we've looked everywhere we can," Bert said. "We might as well go back home."

But Ethan was looking with interest at the big building closest to them.

"That's the seat," he informed Bert.

Bert looked perplexed. "The seat of what?"

"I don't know," Ethan shrugged. "That's what the stationmaster told us. I wonder who lives there?"

Bert surveyed the building carefully. "I don't think anyone does," he decided. Men and women were going in and out the front doors. "It looks more like people work there. Nobody seems to be watching who goes in. Want to go see?"

Since he couldn't think of anyplace else to look for Will, Ethan was more than happy to follow Bert through the large doors.

The boys knew better than to enter a closed room, but if a door stood open, they didn't hesitate to stop and look it over from the hallway. There seemed to be an endless number of things going on in this building. Typewriters clacked and telephones rang. Young men with bundles of papers hurried by. People entered a big room whose swinging doors revealed long rows of seats and a big desk at the front.

"That looks a little like a school," Bert said, "but there ain't no little desks to write on."

"Maybe it's a church where the preacher sits down," Ethan suggested. "But it's sure a lot bigger than our church."

While they stood discussing the possibilities, a smiling woman swung the door open and stepped into the hallway.

"Good morning, boys," she said. "Are you looking for someone?"

"Yes, ma'am," Ethan answered promptly. "My brother."

"Does he work here?"

"Oh, no, ma'am. He's only two years old. He's lost."

"Two years old!" the lady exclaimed. "What makes you think he might be here? How long has he been lost? Where are your parents?"

The questions came so fast that Ethan was unable to

answer. He just stood with his mouth open.

Bert, however, was willing to try.

"He was lost yesterday. We thought maybe—"

At that moment Patterson Quincy walked out of the big room, and stopped to look down at the dusty, barefoot boys.

"Well, well. What have we here, Miss Clark? Are these friends of yours?"

"I've just met them, sir," Miss Clark replied. "They tell me that they've lost a little boy."

"Is that so?" Mr. Quincy fixed his gaze on Ethan and Bert. "Perhaps you'd better tell me about it."

He led the way to an office, and the boys were soon perched uneasily on the edge of chairs in a big room. Mr. Quincy settled behind his desk.

"Now. Let's hear what's going on. Suppose you tell me first where you live."

"At the Briars, sir." Bert answered.

Mr. Quincy was surprised. "At Briarlane Children's Home? And whom did you say you've lost?"

"My little brother, sir," Ethan said. "Yesterday."

"And what is your name?"

"Ethan. Ethan Cooper."

Cooper. Wasn't that the name of the four new children at the home? Patterson Quincy thought that it was.

"Mr. Lehman knows about this, does he?"

"Yes, sir. He's looking for Will now. We thought maybe. . . ." Ethan stopped. He'd better not tell this man their suspicions. They didn't even know who he was. They could get into trouble.

"Shall I see that the boys get back to the Home, Judge Quincy?" Miss Clark asked.

Judge Quincy! Bert and Ethan looked at each other in dismay. That was the name of the lady they were trying to find. If the matron of her house told the judge that they had been there, they were already in trouble.

Mr. Quincy thought for a minute. "No, Miss Clark. Thank you. I believe I'll take them out myself. I'd better look into this matter."

Ethan's shoulders drooped. Would his problems never end? Mr. Lehman would have to know what they had done without permission, and they were no closer to finding Will than they had been.

Slowly the boys followed Mr. Quincy out of the building. It would be a long walk back to the Home.

To their happy surprise, they found they were not going to walk. At the rear of the building stood the limousine, attended by Gridley. Bert stopped with a happy exclamation.

"That's the big car, Ethan! That's the one she came in!"

Mr. Quincy looked perplexed. "You've seen this car before?"

"Oh, yes, sir," Bert replied eagerly. "The lady came with this man. Twice." He pointed at Gridley, who looked neither right nor left.

Thoughtfully Patterson ushered the two boys into the car. Why had Eugenia—it had to be Eugenia—gone to the Home? Why hadn't she mentioned it to him? Gridley had said nothing about such a trip. But then, Mr. Quincy thought, he wouldn't expect him to. Mrs. Quincy had access to the car whenever she wished. He turned his attention to the excited boys.

"We never rode in a fine car like this before!" Bert exclaimed.

"We never rode in no car before," Ethan corrected him. "Wait 'til the guys see us come home like this!"

Bert sat back with a sober look on his face. Now that they were approaching the Briars, he began to reflect on the fact that they had not let anyone know that they were leaving this morning, nor had they asked if they might go. They were sure of punishment from Matron. What might come from Mr. Lehman, he didn't want to imagine.

Mr. Quincy noticed the sudden quiet and hurried to reassure them.

"It's all right, boys. I'll talk to Mr. Lehman when we get there. Perhaps you'd better tell me what you know. When did you say you last saw your little brother?"

"Yesterday. He was there at breakfast. Then we went to paint the henhouses. . . . " Ethan choked as he thought about what else he had painted.

Bert took up the story. "Then when we got back, Matron said she thought Will was with us. But we hadn't seen him."

Mr. Quincy nodded. "So you thought he might have wandered off toward town."

"No, we thought that Mis— that maybe someone took him away, and we'd see him there."

"Chances are he's back by now," Mr. Quincy encouraged

them. "If not, we'll soon find him, I'm sure."

The car stopped in front of the gate, and the boys tumbled out. Unfortunately, there were no children in sight to note their arrival in style. Quickly they ran toward the barn to find Otis.

Patterson Quincy walked slowly toward the building. Several things about this situation disturbed him. How long ago was it that Eugenia had mentioned wanting a child from here? A couple of weeks, he thought. And if he recalled correctly, it was a young Cooper boy that she had specified.

But that was ridiculous. He had convinced her that there was no possibility of such a thing, and nothing more had been said about it. That it might be this child who was missing was coincidental. If Eugenia had visited here— twice—there would be an obvious explanation. George Lehman would straighten it out.

Mr. Quincy's thoughts had carried him to the door, and he was admitted into the dim, cool hall. Mr. Lehman had soon seated his guest in front of the desk. Mr. Quincy looked at the director keenly.

"You look worried, George. Anything wrong?"

"Yes, there is. Quite wrong. The youngest of the new family of children has been missing since some time yesterday. We have carefully searched the house area, the woods, and even the river. There is no sign of him. I sent one of the older boys into town just a little while ago with a message for you. I don't know how he could have gotten there already."

"Probably hasn't," Mr. Quincy responded, and he told Mr. Lehman about the two small boys who had delivered the message by accident. "They didn't know who I was—they just wandered into the courthouse. I told them I'd square things with you so that they wouldn't be in trouble."

Mr. Lehman smiled slightly. "They won't be punished. I know how worried Ethan has been. The boy is just like a father to the other three, and he's not much older than they are. In fact . . ." Mr. Lehman looked distressed.

"Yes?"

"I suspect that the father may have come by and taken the baby with him. We've not been able to locate the man, and have no idea what part of the country he may be in. As I explained to your wife, we have done our best to find him so that the children may be released for adoption or returned home. So far, we've had no success."

"Mmm, yes." Patterson Quincy looked troubled. "You say that you've talked to Mrs. Quincy? Was that about this child who is missing?"

"Why, yes. I thought you knew about it. I didn't mean to divulge a confidence."

"No, no. That's all right. Eugenia has just forgotten to mention it to me. She'll no doubt bring it up when she returns."

"Mrs. Quincy is out of town?" George Lehman made the inquiry out of courtesy, although the less he knew about Eugenia Quincy's affairs, the better he liked it.

"Yes. She has gone to the summer home on the lake this week. Left yesterday."

Suddenly a dreadful possibility clicked into place in Patterson's mind, and he rose abruptly. Startled, Mr. Lehman stood up too.

"You've done what you can do," Mr. Quincy said to him. "I'll start someone out trying to locate the boy immediately. Don't worry. We'll find him."

Patterson's eyes swept over the director's desk.

"We'll get a telephone out here right away," he said. "Can't have people running between here and my office when you need me. I'll be in touch with you soon."

Very soon, he thought grimly as he headed for the car, if what he strongly suspected turned out to be fact. Eugenia couldn't have picked up that boy and taken him with her, could she? As he settled into the car behind a silent Gridley, he berated himself for not being more alert.

"Let's go home, Gridley. We have a trip ahead of us this afternoon."

10

EUGENIA GROWS UP

On the spacious veranda of the summerhouse, Eugenia Quincy lay on a chaise lounge and looked out over the lake. On her first day of what was to be a change of scenery for her, she was tired. Her eyes followed the progress of Clara and the small boy who walked beside her along the water's edge.

After thinking over the events of the previous day, Eugenia wondered uneasily if she had done the right thing. Very soon after they had reached the open road yesterday, Will had fallen asleep on Clara's lap. Eugenia was pleased.

"He's going to be very easy to take care of, Clara," she said happily. "I guess children that age sleep a lot. Have you ever had charge of a baby like him?"

"No, mum," the girl replied. "I was the youngest in my family." She hesitated, then inquired, "What do we feed him?"

Eugenia hadn't considered that. "Why, I suppose

whatever we eat. I'm sure Greta has put in enough for all of us. He can't eat a whole lot."

This, she soon discovered, was the understatement of the day. Will wouldn't eat anything. Shortly after their arrival at the lake, Will had awakened, and seeing only strange faces, had begun to cry. "Allie. Will wants Allie," he sobbed.

"What's allie?" Eugenia asked anxiously. "Is it something to eat? Give him a cookie, Clara."

The cookie was offered, but Will pushed it away.

"Where's Ethan? Where's Allie?" He looked around frantically, and huge tears ran down his face.

"For goodness' sake, Clara. Give him whatever he wants. We can't have that wailing all afternoon."

"I don't know what he wants, mum," Clara replied desperately. "He probably misses his family. Oh, mum! We shouldn't have taken him away from the Home."

"Well, we did, so we'll have to make the best of it. Find something to cheer him up. He's making me nervous."

Clara had done her best, Eugenia was forced to admit, but Will found no happiness in the situation. Throughout the afternoon he continued to cry, adding "Simon" to his list of grievances. When he had finally sobbed himself to sleep again, Eugenia was relieved.

"Well, that's over. Do they all do that, Clara?"

"I don't know, mum. But they all need clean clothes, and we don't have any of those."

"Oh, dear." Eugenia flopped down on the sofa and put her hand on her forehead. "I'm getting a terrible headache, Clara. You'll have to take care of it. Go and get some."

Without opening her eyes, she waved her hand feebly at
the girl. When Clara didn't move, she sat up in surprise.

"Well, what are you waiting for? You'd better go before
he wakes up again. You certainly don't expect me to do
anything with him."

"I never bought little boy's clothes before, mum. And I
got no way to get to the village. And we can't both go
unless we take him with us."

"Oh, bother," Eugenia grumbled. "Why didn't you think
of that before we got here?"

Clara remained silent, knowing that whatever she
answered, it was sure to be the wrong thing.

"I suppose I'll have to go. There's probably not a thing
in that village for a child to wear."

Eugenia flung herself out of the house, muttering about
inefficient help, and headed for the little store that was
closest to the lake. She returned some time later, bearing a
shirt and short pants. They were obviously several sizes too
large, but she threw them down on the table.

"There. When he wakes up you can put them on him."

Clara looked at the outfit dubiously. "Where's the
underwear, mum?"

"Underwear?"

"Yes, mum. He needs more underpants and an undershirt.
The ones he's wearing are . . . sort of wet."

Eugenia was horrified. "Didn't you take him to the
bathroom?"

"He's been asleep, mum. Did you want me to wake him
up?"

"No, no. Of course not. He'll start howling again." She sighed irritably. "I'll have to go back. I certainly wish you could think of things like that before I run myself to a frazzle. You don't have anything else to do."

"Yes, mum. I'm sorry, mum."

"You should be. I brought you along to be of some help."

The rest of the afternoon—and the night—had not gone any better. Several times Eugenia had heard the boy cry, and then was forced to listen to the creak of the rocking chair until he fell asleep again. No wonder she was so fatigued this morning. Aside from a few hiccuping sobs, Will had not cried since Clara had gotten him up. But he still refused to eat.

Eugenia moved restlessly on the chaise lounge. This was not the way she had pictured her advent into motherhood. The boy regarded her solemnly, with a small thumb firmly planted in his mouth. Although he had stopped asking for "Allie" or "Ethan," his big eyes held a disapproving look which was disconcerting to Eugenia.

"What else could he possibly want?" she demanded of Clara. "He won't eat, and he's only taken a little bit of milk. Don't children eat three meals a day like everyone else?"

"Yes, mum. I think so," Clara replied. Her eyes were heavy with lack of sleep, and she was bouncing Will on her knee in an attempt to entertain him. "Maybe he's homesick, mum. Maybe we should take him back to the Briars."

Eugenia considered this and shook her head.

"We can't do that. Mr. Quincy would wonder why we

returned so soon." She looked sharply at Clara. "I don't want him to know about this—not yet at any rate."

"Yes, mum."

"So take the boy down to the lake for a walk. Take a spoon to dig in the sand—or something."

"Yes, mum."

It was going to be a long two or three days ahead. She couldn't force her attention on reading or handwork when she had to be concerned about the child.

Eugenia didn't have long to indulge in self-pity. A crunch on the driveway announced the arrival of a familiar limousine, and she sprang to her feet. The door opened and Gridley stepped out.

"Good afternoon, madam."

"Good afternoon. What . . . ?"

Gridley held open the rear door, and Patterson Quincy emerged and walked toward the veranda.

"Good day, my dear."

"Patterson! What are you doing here? I thought you were too busy to get away!" Eugenia did her best to hide her dismay.

"I found that I had a short time free. I shall have to return this evening, but I wanted to check and see that all was well here."

He ascended the stairs deliberately and sank into a chair beside the chaise lounge.

"Lie down again, Eugenia. You look exhausted." Patterson nodded and looked around with seeming indifference. The trees rustled slightly in the breeze, and the lake glistened in the afternoon sun. He watched the water for a moment in silence.

"Isn't that Clara walking along the shore?" he asked finally.

"Why, yes, I believe it is."

"And who does she have with her? It looks like a small boy."

She made no answer.

"Eugenia?"

She had thought to face him defiantly, but when she raised her eyes to meet his, her face crumpled.

"Eugenia, why on earth did you bring that boy up here without letting anyone know you had him? Don't you realize that you could be prosecuted for kidnapping?"

"Kidnapping!" Eugenia was horrified. "I didn't kidnap him! I just borrowed him for a few days. I was going to take him back."

"Didn't you think that the people at the Home would be looking for him 'for a few days'?"

"Oh, Patterson! He's an orphan. They've got more of those than they need now. And I did ask Mr. Lehman if I might take him, to get acquainted, you know."

"And what did Mr. Lehman say?"

Eugenia tossed her head disdainfully. "Oh, he said he thought the boy was too little to be away from people he knew, but I didn't agree with him. The child is too young to know the difference." Even as she spoke, Eugenia recalled the boy's tearstained face and the fact that he had not eaten since their arrival.

"Nevertheless," Patterson said, "he must be returned as quickly as possible. The people at the Home, and especially his older brother, are frantic over his disappearance."

"Oh, very well. Send Gridley down to the lake to get him and you can take him back with you."

"No, Eugenia. I will not take him and make explanations for you. This is your responsibility, and I suggest that you undertake it immediately." He rose and started for the car.

"Patterson!" Eugenia gasped. "I can't do that! What will I say? Besides, I'm quite sure that Mr. Lehman dislikes me."

"Are you, my dear? I wonder why."

Gridley closed the door of the limousine, and Patterson leaned out the window to speak to his wife.

"If I were you I would start at once. I'll see you at dinner."

Eugenia watched as the car turned on the road leading back to Briarlane. She was furious at Patterson for putting her in this position. She was angry with George Lehman for refusing her permission to take the child when she requested it. If he had not been so stubborn, this never would have happened.

She stormed down to the edge of the lawn to summon Clara. If the girl had seen the car, she would know that Eugenia had been ordered home. How humiliating this was!

"Get our things together, Clara," Eugenia snapped. "We're leaving. We'll take the boy back to the orphanage where he belongs." She looked at Will with disfavor. "I can't have him starving to death when he's in my care. I don't understand why you find it so difficult to get food into a two-year-old child." She gestured impatiently. "Well, move along! We haven't all day to stand around."

"Yes, mum. If you'll watch the boy, I'll pack the car."

"Put him in the chair on the veranda. I'll see that he

doesn't fall out. But hurry. If he starts to cry, you'll have to come and get him."

Dreadful child! Eugenia thought. If they were all like that, she was fortunate not to have any. It would be a relief to get rid of him.

That was another matter which called for serious thought. What was she going to say to Mr. Lehman? As soon as everyone was packed into the car and they were on the road, Eugenia gave it her full attention.

Perhaps she could set Will on the inside of the fence where she had picked him up and go on home. This idea was abandoned almost as soon as it was formed. Patterson was sure to demand a full accounting this evening, and she knew what he would say if he discovered that she hadn't faced George Lehman. Patterson was a kind man, but his sense of justice was spread evenly over everyone, including his wife.

As the miles went by, nothing acceptable came to mind. She pictured George Lehman's face if she simply announced that she had taken the boy out of the yard, and her husband made her bring him back. It was unthinkable . . . but no explanation occurred to her that would not bring the blame squarely down upon her own head.

There was no sound from the backseat. Probably the boy had fallen asleep again. He didn't have to have a story ready to explain his disappearance. When the car stopped in front of the gate, Eugenia was no closer to a solution than when they had left the lake. Reluctantly she stepped out of the car, removed her driving gloves, and laid them on the seat. Followed by Clara with a sleeping Will in her arms, she began the long trek to the door of the Briars.

The next few moments were a blur of activity. The girl who opened the door took in the scene, then shrieked. "Will! Here's Will! He's back!" and ran to summon Matron.

The noise brought Mr. Lehman rushing to the hallway. Before Eugenia could open her mouth, he was shaking her hand and smiling broadly.

"Oh, Mrs. Quincy! You've found him! You'll never know how grateful we are to you. His brothers and sister have been so upset—as we all have—and you've brought him back. How can I ever thank you?"

Relief caused Eugenia to lean weakly against the wall. That was it, of course. She had found the child wandering in the road and had brought him back. Everyone was happy, and that was the end of the matter.

Will had awakened and was crying again. His eager stranglehold on Matron when she took him from Clara's arms brought unexpected tears to Eugenia's eyes.

"Mr. Lehman, I wish to speak with you a moment if I may," she said.

"Of course." He ushered her into his office and closed the door.

When Eugenia emerged some time later, her face was white, but calm. For the first time in her life Eugenia Quincy had admitted to herself—and to someone else— that she had been wrong. And she had misjudged George Lehman. He had been most understanding and forgiving. Now she would go home and throw herself on the mercy of the court.

11

HUGH MAKES
A DEMAND

Will was the center of attention at supper that evening. Although he allowed the children to hug him, he would not leave the security of Matron's lap. He ate everything offered to him, including an extra pudding. Matron finally had to call a halt.

"He's going to be sick all night if you feed him any more," she laughed. "I know we're glad to have him back, but let's save some of the celebration for tomorrow."

"Where'd ya go, Will?" Simon asked him. "How'd ya get out the gate?"

Of course Will couldn't tell him. His only comment was "pretty car." Bert put the story together quickly.

"He went for a ride someplace, that's for sure. And how many cars have you seen around here?"

"Only the big one," Ethan replied. "But Mr. Quincy would've known if he was in that one. I still think he went with Mrs. Quincy. I'm going to watch him from now on, in case she decides to come back."

"We mustn't forget to thank the Lord for bringing Will home safely," Matron said as they prepared for bed that night.

Ethan was surprised. "How do we do that?"

"The same way we asked Him to take care of Will," Matron replied. "We'll thank Him when we pray."

"I guess Matron was right," Ethan confided to Bert later. "It is a good idea to pray about stuff. Do you think the Lord really does have His eye on us every minute?"

Bert thought this was true. "I heard it in Sunday school, and Matron told us the same thing. She read it in the Bible, so it must be so."

Ethan recalled Ma telling them some stories from the Bible. Apparently there were more that he hadn't heard yet.

"Bert, doesn't it make you nervous to think of Someone watching you all the time?"

"It does if I'm doing something wrong," Bert replied.

"What happens if you do something wrong, and He sees you?"

Bert thought this over for a moment.

"Well, if I wish I hadn't done it, I say I'm sorry and I won't do it again. Then He forgives me. Matron says the two most important things to say are 'thank you' and 'I'm sorry.'"

"God sure has a lot of people to watch," Ethan said with a sigh. "I hope He doesn't miss anyone."

One person at the Home who didn't seem to worry

about God watching him was Hugh. He did all he could to make life miserable for the younger children, but no one dared report him to Matron or to Mr. Lehman.

For his part, Ethan kept out of Hugh's way as much as possible. Yet more and more often he found himself finishing Hugh's chores or taking on a disagreeable task when Hugh reminded him of what might happen to boys who knew more than they should.

"How long has Hugh been around here?" Ethan asked Bert. "He acts like he owns the place."

"Just about all his life, I guess," Bert replied. "Him and Riley been here the longest of any." He looked at Ethan sharply. "You ain't lit into him again, have you?"

"Naw. He can do what he wants to me, but he better not touch my brothers or Alice. What makes him so mean, anyway?"

"He's probably mad 'cause no one adopted him," Bert replied. "I remember he had a chance to be farmed out once, but he said if he just had to clean another barn, he'd rather stay with this one."

As the days went on and it came time to think of school beginning, Hugh became more sullen. He was overheard to declare, "I ain't going back to that school again. I'm big enough to get me a job and earn some money."

"Mr. Lehman won't let you quit school," Riley pointed out to him. "And you have to live someplace. If you go to work on another farm, you might not get any more than you do here—your room and board."

"I ain't going to be no farmer," Hugh replied. "I'm

going to be a . . . a banker!"

"A banker!" Riley hooted. "You, a banker?" Then seeing the scowl on Hugh's face, he added quickly, "Of course, you are the best one in school in arithmetic. No one else can do problems in his head like you can. Instead of quitting, you should get ready for high school. Then when you graduate, you could get a job in a bank."

Hugh shook his head. "That takes too long. I got to get away now."

"You ain't thinking of running away, are you?" Riley said. "I wouldn't do that if I were you. You might not ever have it as easy as this again."

"I'll take my chances," Hugh growled.

Riley left him to his thoughts, and Hugh sat watching the younger boys play in the field. When the ball rolled in his direction, he picked it up and held it until Ethan came running after it.

"Here, kid," he said. "You want this back?"

Ethan nodded and held out his hand.

"You gotta pay me for it."

Ethan backed away. "I don't have any money."

"I'm not talking about money. You gotta do something for me."

"What?"

"I'll tell you later. You gonna promise, or do I have to talk to Mr. Lehman?"

"I . . . I guess so," Ethan stammered. "But what if I can't do it?"

"You can do it all right. You just have to keep your

mouth shut. And if I can't trust you . . ." Hugh left the rest of the threat unsaid, but Ethan knew what it would be.

"You can trust me," he declared. "I haven't said anything yet, have I?"

"And you better not. I'll see you later." Hugh tossed the ball in Ethan's direction and turned toward the barn.

Ethan ran back to the game, but his heart was no longer in it.

"What's that big bully want now?" Bert inquired. "Do you have to finish his chores?"

"Naw. He didn't say what he wanted. He just talks a lot." Ethan pretended that nothing was wrong, but the big lump in his stomach told him that something dreadful lay ahead.

It was not long in coming. Ethan's morning chore was dusting the parlor and hallway and emptying the waste baskets—the job that had been Bert's the day he met Mrs. Quincy at the door. As Ethan worked, the big front door opened slightly and Hugh beckoned him out to the steps.

After looking around carefully, Hugh whispered, "I came to tell you what I want you to do. Remember, you promised. You need to do it now."

Ethan was alarmed. "I have to finish my chores or I'll be in trouble with Matron! I can't leave 'til she checks."

"You don't even have to stop working," Hugh said. "Have you emptied the trash baskets yet?"

Ethan shook his head. "You want me to empty the ones upstairs, too?"

Hugh looked disgusted. "Naw—why would I want that?

I want you to wait until Mr. Lehman goes out to talk to Otis before you get the wastebasket in the office. Now listen. In the little drawer in the top of Mr. Lehman's desk is a box. It has something in it that . . . that belongs to me. Just drop the little box in the wastebasket and bring it out to the back with the rest of the stuff. I'll take care of it from there."

Ethan's face turned white. "Open Mr. Lehman's desk? I can't do that! I don't even dust his desk. And he's always there when I take the trash."

"Keep your voice down! He won't be there today because Otis just sent someone to get him. By the time he gets back, you'll be all through here and gone. Now, you gonna do what I told you, or not?"

Ethan shook his head. "I never took anything in my life, and I'm sure not going to steal from Mr. Lehman. You can do whatever you want to me, but I won't do that."

Hugh was angry. "Might have known you wouldn't be any good. You can't even keep a promise. I guess we'll have to see if Mr. Lehman believes you never stole nothing when I tell him about what you took from Riley's cupboard. You'll be sorry!"

Hugh ran down the steps and around the building, and Ethan hurried back into the hallway. He would get the basket from Mr. Lehman's office at once, before Mr. Lehman left. Then the director would know that he hadn't touched anything. But when Ethan reached the office and pushed open the door, Mr. Lehman's chair was empty. He had already left to see Otis. Now what? Should he risk

Matron's disfavor by leaving his job undone, or rush in and get the basket as fast as he could?

To his great relief, Matron's voice spoke behind him. "Aren't you finished yet, Ethan? What's taking you so long?"

"Mr. Lehman isn't here, and I didn't know if I should go in."

Matron walked in and looked around. "That's odd. He never leaves his office unlocked when he goes out. He must have left in a big hurry." She turned to Ethan and patted his shoulder.

"You were right, Ethan. We don't enter the office unless Mr. Lehman is here. Let me get the basket for you, then I'll put the lock on the door."

She brought the basket out, then turned to push the lock. "No, better not," she muttered. "If he left that fast, he may not have his keys. We'll just close the door and leave it."

Ethan followed Matron to the kitchen. While he was grateful that she had come so that he didn't have to make a decision, he was worried about what Hugh would do next. Should he tell Matron what Hugh had asked him to do? No, she might think he had been on his way in when she appeared! Besides, Ethan didn't trust Hugh not to harm his brothers or Alice. He'd better keep it to himself. When Hugh went to Mr. Lehman, Ethan would have to explain things the best he could and hope that Mr. Lehman would believe him.

Life was hard, Ethan decided. If he only had himself to worry about, it wouldn't be so bad, but he had three others depending on him. He couldn't do anything to get them sent away.

"We ain't got much longer to do this," Bert remarked as he and Ethan sat fishing on the river's edge that afternoon. "School starts next month. You been to school much?"

"Yeah, some," Ethan replied. "I had to stay home to help Ma when she was sick. But I know how to read and write, and I can do some numbers. Will I be in your grade?"

"Probably. You're eight and so am I." Bert reflected on the future. "I like school pretty much. Course, some of the guys call us 'Thorny,' but I don't pay any attention to that."

" 'Thorny'? Why do they call you that?"

" 'Cause we're from the Briars," Bert explained. "Some kids from here don't like to be teased, but it doesn't bother me. The town kids found out that you don't call Shala that more than once. She can use her fists as good as any boy. They stay away from her."

Ethan understood that. But before he could open his mouth to say so, someone crashed through the bushes behind them and ran to the river. Almost as though she had heard her name, Shala appeared and plunked herself down beside the surprised boys.

"It's getting kind of crowded in this spot," Bert said in disgust. "Let's go down the river, Ethan."

"Wait," Shala panted. "Wait 'til I get my breath. I was sent down to get you."

"What's the matter? Is Will gone again?" Ethan jumped to his feet in alarm.

Shala shook her head. "Will's fine. He's with Matron.

Mr. Lehman wants to talk to everyone together, so you have to come back now."

"What's he going to talk about?" Bert asked as they hurried toward the house.

"I don't know," Shala replied. "He just said round everybody up. So I came after you."

"How'd you know where we were?" Bert demanded suspiciously.

"I saw you start out with your fishing poles. I figured you weren't on the way to the orchard to pick apples."

"Smarty," Bert muttered. "You better not be trying to fool us."

The boys joined the other children in the dining room just before a solemn-looking Mr. Lehman came in.

"Something very serious has happened here today," he said. "A box containing some money belonging to the Home is missing from my desk. I am not accusing anyone here of taking it. I am hoping it was just misplaced. I only want to ask all of you to keep watch around the house and the barn. If you see any strangers, let one of us know right away."

Mr. Lehman said a few more things, but Ethan wasn't listening. His heart had dropped to his shoes. Could that be the box Hugh wanted him to get? Did Hugh go back and get it himself after Ethan and Matron had left? If so, he would surely tell Mr. Lehman that Ethan had taken it. Should he try to talk to Hugh about it?

As carefully as he could, Ethan looked around the room for the older boy. Hugh was nowhere to be seen.

12

THE SUMMER ENDS

By bedtime everyone knew that Hugh was gone.

"Are we going to ask the Lord to bring him back, like we did Will?" Ethan asked when Matron came to pray with him.

"We'll certainly ask the Lord to protect Hugh and be with him," Matron replied. "I don't reckon he's in danger as a little boy would be. He can pretty well take care of himself, but I don't like to see him leave the Home before he finishes school. This is the only family Hugh has ever had."

After Matron had turned out the light and left, Bert questioned Riley.

"Do you know where Hugh went, Riley?"

"Nope."

"Do you think he'll be back?"

"Dunno."

"Did he tell you he was going?"

"Not exactly. He said he didn't want to go back to school. He wanted to get a job and earn some money."

"If they find him, will they bring him back?"

"Maybe, maybe not," Riley replied. "If he got himself apprenticed somewhere, likely Mr. Lehman would let him stay. He only had another year to be ready to go on his own."

Ethan hoped that Hugh would not return. Even though he was not in sight, Ethan still worried that Hugh would carry out his threat to go to Mr. Lehman. He knew that Hugh had been angry with him this morning.

Ethan stirred restlessly in his bed. He was the only one with the knowledge that Hugh knew about the box. If only there were someone he could tell about it without getting into trouble. Suddenly his eyes flew open.

If the Lord were watching him every minute, Ethan reasoned, He would be listening, too! Ethan could tell Him. This was a comforting thought. After explaining to the Lord all that had happened that day, Ethan felt much better. He wouldn't tell Mr. Lehman what he knew, Ethan decided. He would let the Lord do that.

Hugh didn't appear the next day, nor the day after. As Matron bustled around preparing school clothes for the children, she looked sad.

"I think Matron really misses old Hugh," Ethan remarked. "I don't see why. I'm glad he's gone."

"So am I," Bert agreed. "But we haven't known him as long as Matron has. He was younger than Will when he came here."

"How come he grew up to be so ornery? Didn't he want people to like him?"

"Yeah, prob'ly," Bert replied. "But he found out that nobody did when other kids got adopted and he stayed. Now he's too old for anyone to want him." Bert thoughtfully chewed on a straw. "I can sorta see how he feels."

Ethan glanced at his friend. "How come you're not ornery?"

Bert grinned. "I like it here. I don't want anybody to adopt me, 'cause my folks might come back. They'd be awful disappointed if I was gone. If they don't show up by the time I'm sixteen, I'll hunt for 'em. How about you? Are you going to look for your pa?"

Ethan shook his head. "I have to stay until Will is sixteen," he said. "I promised Russell I'd look after the little kids."

"Guess you'll never be adopted, then. Not many folks want four at one time."

There was no opportunity to worry about that the day before school began. The boys were informed that haircuts would start directly after breakfast. A tall stool was placed in the backyard, and one by one they submitted to the draped towel and the cold scissors wielded by Matron.

"Look at all the extra neck we have to wash," Bert moaned. "And it ain't even the same color as the rest of us.

Now Matron can tell if we forgot behind our ears."

He advised Ethan to ignore the snickers and remarks from the girls, but Ethan blushed when Shala pointed out his "rooster tail" and suggested that he put his head under the pump and plaster the hair down.

Nevertheless, he was excited about beginning school. "I won't have to stay home 'cause someone's sick," he confided to Bert. "I can go to school every day."

The next day he held firmly to Alice's hand, though the others raced on ahead. The older girls offered to escort Alice safely to the schoolhouse, but Ethan declined.

"This is her first day," he explained. "I need to make sure she isn't scared or anything. Tomorrow she can go with you."

Alice chatted happily as they walked along.

"Will I get books to take home like the big kids have, Ethan?"

"Yeah, sure. You'll have some books."

"Will I be able to read them tonight?"

Ethan smiled at her. "Not all of them. You may learn some words today, but it takes a while to be able to read a whole book."

Alice sighed happily. "At least I'll be able to carry them in my book bag." She skipped a little to keep up with Ethan. "I already have a pencil box in there. And a clean hankie that Matron gave me. And an apple for recess."

"Mmm. That's nice." Ethan listened with only half an ear, answering when it seemed appropriate. The others were ahead of them, and he was anxious to get there in time for a game of stickball before classes started. Alice had to run to keep up with him.

"Will you open it for me?" she asked.

"Open what?"

"My pencil box! I just told you!"

"Sure, remind me when we get home this afternoon, and I'll do it."

Alice stopped in the road and pulled on Ethan's arm.

"Ethan, I told you it had lots of pencils in it and I need them for school! You have to do it now."

Ethan could see children running toward the schoolhouse as the bell began to ring.

"I can't, Alice. See? The kids are all going in, and we'll be late if we don't run. Here, let me carry your bag. I'll open the box at recess."

Alice was assigned to the primer class. After an examination, Ethan joined the third reader with Bert. Mr. Smalley welcomed everyone to a new year and began the process of handing out books. Alice beamed with delight as the primer, speller, and arithmetic book were given to her.

Ethan had already been told that only girls carried book bags. The boys had straps to hold their books together. Even so, he was not prepared for the number that were handed out.

". . . four, five, six, seven! Do we really have to learn all this?"

"Yep," Bert replied. "Don't worry about it. Matron helps with studying in the evening. Just pay attention here and you won't have any trouble."

Ethan wasn't sure about that, but he determined to do

his best. For a moment he thought how proud Ma would be that he was in school. Maybe his older brothers and sisters would like to know too. He'd ask Matron to help him write a letter to them.

Lessons were assigned, and everyone settled down to work. When the primer class was called to the front of the room, Ethan looked up to watch Alice walk proudly to the bench beside the teacher's desk. The seat she had been sitting in was directly in front of him, four rows ahead. Ethan glanced at her desk, and his eyes widened in horror.

What was that on her desk? It certainly did not hold pencils! No wonder Alice couldn't get the box open. It was made of metal and was fastened with a lock. As he stared at the box in fascination, Ethan knew exactly what it was and where it had come from, even though he had never seen it. It was the box of money from Mr. Lehman's desk.

How had Alice gotten it? She couldn't have taken it from the office.

Ethan forgot about the books in front of him. His mind was in a whirl. Somehow he had to get that box and hide it from sight. He started to get up, but Bert tugged on his overall strap.

"You can't walk around without permission," he whispered. "Where ya going?"

Ethan sat back down. There was nothing he could do while the whole room looked on. At recess he'd get the box. By then maybe he'd think what to do with it.

He looked around cautiously to see if anyone else had noticed, but everyone seemed to be reading. Fortunately the older students were in the next room. One of them would certainly recognize the box, and then there would be a lot of explaining to do. The Coopers would be sent away at once.

There was still a lot of explaining to do, Ethan decided as he waited for recess time. Was there any way to get the money box back to the office without anyone knowing?

As soon as the children were dismissed for play, Ethan rushed to the front of the room. "Alice, go get your book bag from the coatroom."

"Why?"

"Because I want to put your . . . your pencil box in it. We have to take it back home."

"Why?" Alice wailed. "It's mine. Matron said I could keep it. I want the pencils out of it!"

"Don't cry," Ethan said. "Look. I have to take it home to get it open. See? There's nothing here at school to take the lock off. Here, you can have my pencil today. All right?"

Alice was reluctant, but Ethan was finally able to persuade her to give him the box. Quickly he crammed it into the book bag. Now what would he do with it? He couldn't leave the bag in the coatroom, out of sight. What if some other girl took it by mistake, or looked into it at lunchtime?

There was nothing to do but keep it with him. That meant that he wouldn't be able to go outside to play all day. Wearily he returned to his desk and put the bag at his feet.

At morning recess the happy sounds of laughter and games floated in through the open window. Once again, through no fault of his own, Ethan wasn't a part of the fun. If only he had just himself to take care of, life would be a lot easier.

The rest of the morning dragged on slowly. Ethan's class had not been called to recite, so he had no reason to leave his seat. At noon, however, he was faced with a dilemma.

"Come on, Ethan. Get your dinner pail and come outside to eat," Bert said.

"Uh, I guess I'll eat in here," Ethan replied. "You go ahead."

Bert regarded him with suspicion. "What's the matter with you? You never came out for recess. You stuck to that desk or something?"

"Naw," Ethan mumbled. "I think I'll do some extra reading this noon. Tomorrow I'll go out with you." He pulled a book from his desk and flipped it open.

"You gonna read the arithmetic book?" Bert shook his head in disbelief as he made his way to the door.

After looking forward to school all summer, Ethan thought as he munched his sandwich, this certainly was not what he had envisioned. His head ached over the problem of what to do about that pesky box. Any way he looked at it, Ethan could foresee only trouble for the Coopers. What if Mr. Lehman sent him away and made the others stay there? Where had Alice gotten hold of that box, anyway?

The first class after lunch was penmanship. Ethan sat with his copybook open in front of him and hoped that no one would notice him.

"Ethan?" Mr. Smally's voice seemed to echo through the room as he spoke.

"Yes, sir?"

"You're not writing your exercise."

"No, sir."

"I presume you have a good reason for not doing this lesson."

Ethan sank lower into his seat. His face was red as all eyes turned in his direction.

"Yes, sir. I don't have a pencil."

"I see." Mr. Smalley glared at the giggling boys and girls. "And how did you expect to do your work without the proper tools?"

Ethan opened his mouth to answer when Alice spoke for him. "He gave his pencil to me." Then she added proudly, "He's my brother."

"That is commendable, I'm sure." Mr. Smalley said. "Perhaps you'd let him borrow it this afternoon." He looked at Ethan. "Tomorrow it would be well to provide one for each of you."

"Yes, sir," Ethan gulped, bending his head over his copybook. Would this day never end? At least when school was out he'd be safe from discovery until he could decide what to do next.

When they were finally dismissed, Ethan strapped his books together, then picked up Alice's book bag. He was determined to hang on to it until they got home.

"You gonna carry her bag every day?" Bert wanted to know. "The guys will tease you for sure."

"She can carry it tomorrow," Ethan replied. "This is her first day. It's pretty heavy for a little girl."

Bert was right. The older boys joined them on the walk home, and they were quick to notice what Ethan had.

"Well, look at Mama's boy with the book bag!" one of them called. "Maybe we should help him carry it!"

Before Ethan knew what was coming, the boy grabbed the bag and ran with it.

"Hey! Give that back!" Ethan yelled and started after him.

"Here, Fred—catch it!" The boy threw the bag to one of his companions. In less than a second the worst had happened. The box flew out, hit the ground with a thud, and the contents scattered around in front of the astonished children.

"Boy, oh boy," Bert muttered as he helped Ethan scoop up the money and stuff it into the book bag. "Are you in for it now!"

13

GRIDLEY PICKS UP
A STRANGER

Gridley, the Quincys' driver, stood beside the big touring car and looked up and down the deserted road. This was a most annoying circumstance. If he hadn't taken his eye from the road when a rabbit ran out of the bush, he could have avoided the rock that lay in the center of his path. He winced, remembering the grinding sound of a hole being torn in the crankcase oil pan. By the time he stopped the car, the oil had all run out and soaked into the dusty road.

He could give the hole an emergency repair job, but unfortunately he had neglected to bring a supply of oil. The nearest village was just a mile or so down the road, but it might as well have been ten or twenty miles, for Gridley dared not leave the car to go get it.

He glanced at the sun, then pulled a watch from his pocket. He should have reached the summerhouse by now, where Mr. and Mrs. Quincy awaited the car to bring them home.

Gridley prided himself on the care of his automobiles. How could he have been so thoughtless as to start out without extra oil? Well, he had, and the chances of anyone coming along this back road to rescue him were slim indeed. He sat down on the running board and pondered his alternatives. He had already rejected the thought of abandoning the car. That left waiting for another conveyance or a passerby who would be willing to help him.

The summer evening was cool, and the view from where he sat was pleasant, but Gridley was in no mood to enjoy it. When half an hour had passed with no change in the scenery, he began to pace back and forth. Suddenly across the field, silhouetted against the sunset, there appeared the figure of a man. His head was bent, and he apparently had not seen the car in the road. Gridley watched his approach. He was carrying a knapsack and seemed to be in no hurry. Gridley was about to call to him when the fellow looked up, stopped, then turned as if to go back the way he had come.

Gridley waved his arms frantically. "Hello! Hello, there! Can you help me?"

The figure hesitated, then walked slowly toward the road. As he came nearer, Gridley saw that it was not a man but a young boy.

"I'm having a little trouble here," Gridley said. "If you could go up to the next village and get some oil for the car, I'd make it worth your while."

The boy looked admiringly at the shiny vehicle and rubbed his hand lovingly over the hood.

"Sure, mister. I'll go."

Gridley handed him a bill. "This should do it. I need four quarts of oil. By the way, what's your name?"

"Hugh. Hugh Kelly."

"You live around here?"

"Well, I'm sort of traveling right now."

Gridley looked at the boy closely. Fifteen, maybe sixteen, he figured. Old enough to look out for himself. "All right. You can leave your knapsack here if you like. I'll watch it."

Hugh shook his head. "It's not heavy. I'll take it with me." He turned and trotted off toward the village. Gridley sat down and watched as the boy disappeared around a bend in the road.

That may be the last I'll see of him or the money, he thought. *But it's the only chance I've seen to get out of here.* He leaned against the car and prepared to wait.

Within the hour, Gridley was relieved to see the boy returning.

Hugh handed over the cans of oil and dug in his pocket for the change.

"You can keep that for your trouble," Gridley told him. Hugh's face lit up with pleasure, and Gridley decided that the boy hadn't been in possession of much money in the past.

Gridley poured the oil into the car, then shined the already immaculate engine. "I'm on my way up to Scott Lake," he said. "Can I drop you somewhere?"

Hugh grinned with delight. "I was going that way myself," he said. "I'd be glad to keep you company."

Hugh looked around with pleasure as the car purred along the road. They must be going at least twenty miles an hour, he figured. He'd never ridden that fast in his life. Wait until he told the fellows about this! Then he remembered that he had no intention of returning to the Home. He was on his own.

"So, are you finished with school, Hugh?"

"Yes, sir. I'm through." He looked over at Gridley. The man looked friendly enough. He might as well tell him the truth. "Actually I got another year to go, but I figure I can do better with my life than sitting in a schoolhouse every day."

Gridley nodded. "Do you have a job waiting up this way?"

"Not exactly," Hugh admitted, "but I'm sure I can find one. I'm a good worker. What I need is a place where there aren't a lot of little kids hanging around all the time."

"Oh. Come from a big family, I guess."

"Uh, yeah. I suppose you could say that."

Gridley was pretty sure he knew just how large a "family" Hugh came from. Hugh wasn't the first runaway the Briars had known.

"My boss hires young men to work at the courthouse," Gridley said. "They work as messengers and train to be clerks. I could speak to him about a place for you if you'd like."

Hugh turned to him in disbelief. "You could? You mean you really would?"

"You need to realize that he's a strict boss. You'd have to toe the mark and obey orders."

Hugh nodded happily.

"It would mean you'd have to go back to town, you know. So if you find something up here you'd like more, you'd better take it."

Hugh said nothing, but Gridley noted the look of disappointment on the boy's face. Obviously he had run away from the Home and was reluctant to return.

The conversation turned to other matters, and in half an hour they approached the lake and the summer home. Mr. Quincy met them in the driveway.

"Well, Gridley. Have some trouble along the way, did you?"

"Yes, sir. I hit a rock in the road and had to repair the oil pan. This young fellow was good enough to get more oil for me."

"That so? Well, we appreciate that. Both of you go right to the kitchen. Clara has kept your supper hot. We won't try to go back tonight. Leave first thing in the morning. You can find a bed back there for the young man."

"Yes, sir." Gridley motioned Hugh to follow him and started around the house.

Mr. Quincy stopped him. "What's your name, son?"

"Hugh. Hugh Kelly, sir."

"Kelly. Kelly. Haven't I seen you before?"

"No, sir. I don't think so."

"There's a young boy at the Briars with that name," Mr. Quincy said. "He'd be about your age. You're not that one, are you? No, no. He wouldn't be that far away from home. Go along and eat your supper."

Hugh breathed a sigh of relief and followed Gridley to the kitchen.

"You can take a walk down by the lake," Gridley told him when they had finished eating. "Clara will fix your bed. We'll turn in early tonight."

Hugh nodded and headed for the lake, still carrying his knapsack.

"Don't know what that kid has in that sack that he won't let loose of it," Gridley said to Clara. "Likely everything he owns. He was honest enough not to run off with my money, so he's not likely to have anything that doesn't belong to him."

Hugh sat down by the water and skipped a few stones across the surface. He couldn't believe his good fortune. Not only had he ridden in the greatest car he'd ever seen, but the possibility of a job had been offered to him. He'd never go back to that orphanage again.

As darkness fell, Hugh got up and started back to the house. He had never seen such a fancy place before. Lights shone through the open windows, and he could see Mr. Quincy sitting at a desk. Suddenly his heart seemed to stop beating, for he could hear very clearly what the man was saying.

"Mr. Lehman? Patterson Quincy here. Glad we got that telephone in for you. No, I'm not at home. I'm here at the summer place. . . . You say you've been trying to get me? Something wrong, is there? . . . Um . . . Yes, I see. . . . Any idea how much was in there? . . . I suppose you have no idea who could have taken it? . . . Missing since night before last,

eh? . . . No, of course you don't want to think he'd take it,
but listen, George. Here's a coincidence for you. The boy has
turned up here. My driver picked him up on the road. . . .
Yes, yes. We're coming back in the morning. . . . I'll wait
until we get there to talk to him. . . . Yes. We'll meet in your
office. . . . I'm sure we'll straighten this out. Maybe it will
turn up before then. . . . Yes, see you tomorrow."

Hugh turned away from the window in a panic. What
could he do? Before he could reach a decision, Gridley
rounded the corner and spied him.

"There you are, Hugh. I was just going down to the lake
to get you. Clara has your bed ready. If you've been on the
road since morning, you'll probably be glad for some sleep,
eh?"

"Yes, sir." Hugh walked with Gridley to the small room
at the back of the house. He closed the door and sat down
on the edge of the bed to think.

In the living room, Patterson Quincy had finished his
conversation and sat in thought also.

"You were going to tell Mr. Lehman about the offer
you've had," his wife said. "I didn't hear you mention it."

"Something else came up, Eugenia," Mr. Quincy replied.
"I'll need to visit his office in the morning. We'll discuss it
then. Probably better than trying to explain it over the
telephone."

Eugenia dropped her embroidery in her lap. "Do you
really feel that this plan is a good one, Patterson? Will it be
the best thing for these children?"

"Horton tells me that it has been most successful in

New York City and Chicago. The agents check the homes very carefully before the children are placed in them. The program has been working well for many years now, and we have sufficient time to check it out thoroughly before the next group is made up."

"But a train! I just can't see those little children put on a train and sent way out west by themselves! They'll be frightened to death!"

"They won't be alone, Eugenia," her husband reassured her. "They'll be escorted the whole way. And it's not as though there would be no one expecting them. I understand the advertising is most efficient. It will be the only chance some of these children will ever have to belong to a family."

"You're probably right," Eugenia said. "How many will be taken from the Briars?"

"At least ten. We should begin at once to check the records and choose the most eligible."

"I hope the Cooper children will be among them," Eugenia said. "Is that possible?"

"If we locate the father, or failing that, get permission from the older brother, I would say so. There could be some difficulty in placing four children in one home, but some prosperous farmer might be persuaded to take all of them. They will certainly be considered when we make our decision."

Patterson looked over at his wife. Eugenia had become a different person in the past few weeks. She seemed to have grown older . . . well, maybe not older, but more thoughtful.

There was a difference about her since the incident with the Cooper child. He recalled the day. Dinner that evening had been a silent affair.

"Well, my dear, I presume your interview with Mr. Lehman was satisfactory?" he'd said finally.

"Yes. He was most understanding. Patterson, you were right when you suggested that I was not ready for the responsibility of a child. My reasons for wanting the little boy were selfish ones. I thought of him more as a plaything rather than a son. It would have been a mistake to keep him."

Patterson had been so surprised at this confession that the lecture he had intended to deliver was forgotten. This was a side of Eugenia that he had not been permitted to see before. From that day on she had been less demanding and seemed more contented with her home.

The next morning at the appointed time, Mr. and Mrs. Quincy walked out to the limousine for the ride back to town. Clara had already taken her place in front.

Mr. Quincy looked about. "Where's the young boy, Gridley? Does he know it's time to leave?"

"I don't know, sir. He wasn't in his bed when I went to wake him this morning. It appears he didn't spend the night here after all."

ETHAN TELLS
HIS STORY

A silent group of children gathered around as Ethan and
Bert picked up the last piece of money and put it in Alice's
book bag. No one had offered to help them, even though
some of the bills had blown over into the grass beside the
road.

"I hope we got it all," Bert said. "Do you know how
much was in there?"

Ethan shook his head. "I never saw it before."

"I know you never took it," Bert said. "And we know
that Alice didn't. So how did it get there?"

Ethan had no answer. He could think only about what
needed to be done. He closed the bag securely and grabbed
Alice's hand. After the first cry when the boy had snatched
the book bag, she too had remained silent. Now she hurried
along between Ethan and Bert.

"There weren't any pencils in my box, were there,

Ethan?" Tears rolled down her cheeks. "The teacher said we both had to have one by tomorrow. What will we do?"

"You'll have a pencil, Alice. Don't worry." To himself he thought glumly, *I'm sure I won't be needing mine.*

Bert voiced his thoughts. "The first day of school is usually hard, but I never seen anything like this before. It makes my stomach hurt to think about it. Where did you get that box anyway?"

"I don't know," Ethan answered miserably. "It was in Alice's bag. She said she had a pencil box, and I never saw it until we were in school."

Alice sniffed again. "Matron told me I could keep it," she said.

"Did Matron see the box, Alice?" Bert asked her.

"No. I put it away for school."

"But who gave it to you?"

"Nobody. I found it out by the barn. Otis said he didn't want it." Alice looked anxiously at Ethan. "Are we in trouble?"

"You're not, Alice," her brother replied. "We'll just hope that Mr. Lehman doesn't think I'm the one who left it out there."

"What are you going to do, Ethan?" Bert inquired. "Are we going right to his office as soon as we get home?"

Ethan looked sick. "I suppose I'll have to. Just about every kid in school knows about it. What do you think he'll do?"

Bert shrugged. "I don't know. Nothing like this has ever happened since I've been here. But I never saw Mr. Lehman whip anyone, even when they did something real bad."

"He could send me away."

Bert didn't reply.

The children were met at the door by Matron. "Put your books away and change your clothes, boys," she said. "Otis needs you in the barn for a job, then you can play until supper time. We'll work on your lessons right after you eat."

Ethan pushed the book bag into the cupboard and was grateful for some extra time before he had to face Mr. Lehman. He could not understand, however, why none of the other children were rushing to tell what they'd seen. Several of the onlookers had been from the Home, including Shala.

Ethan mentioned this to Bert, who seemed surprised at the question.

"Nobody tells nothing to Mr. Lehman," he said. "You're expected to take care of stuff yourself. We don't tell on anyone around here."

"You mean if I never told Mr. Lehman about the money he wouldn't ever know?"

"Prob'ly not. But the other kids would know, and they prob'ly wouldn't play with you or nothing."

Ethan thought this over as he did his chores. That meant that Hugh was bluffing him when he threatened to go to the director. Did it also mean that he couldn't tell what he knew about Hugh? Of course it did, he thought. He would not be able to tell Mr. Lehman that Hugh had asked him to get the box from the drawer, and that he had refused.

Ethan decided there was nothing for him to do but take the blame for the whole thing. He couldn't say that Alice found the box. She was too little to be responsible. Besides, it wasn't her fault. It was his for not standing up to Hugh. Whatever punishment was coming belonged to him.

Ethan wasn't hungry for supper. His stomach hurt, and he pushed the food around his plate until Bert noticed and spoke to him.

"You gotta eat your supper or Matron'll think you're sick. Shove it in whether you want it or not. Can I have your cake?"

Ethan nodded and did his best to clear his plate. The hour after mealtime was spent on lessons. Baths and bed followed, and Ethan found himself being prayed with and told good night by Matron before he had had any chance to take care of his problem.

Even though he was tired, Ethan's eyes would not close. He lay still and stared at the ceiling until he was sure the others were asleep. Then as quietly as possible, he crept from his bed and took the box from his cupboard. Silently he tiptoed down the long stairway and into the darkened hall. The office door was open; Ethan could see the light. But when he reached the room and peeked in, he heard Mr. Lehman talking on the telephone.

"The box disappeared from my desk day before yesterday," he was saying. "No, I don't . . . I don't want to suspect any of my children, but . . ."

Ethan heard no more, for he had turned and run swiftly back to the bedroom. His heart beat wildly as he returned the box to his cupboard and went back to bed. Was Mr. Lehman talking to the police? Would Ethan be put in jail? If they found the box while he was in school tomorrow, would they come and get him? Ethan curled up in bed and tried to think what he must do.

In the morning he looked ill, and Matron was concerned. She put her hand on his forehead. "Are you coming down with something, Ethan? We'd better go upstairs and take your temperature."

Ethan sat on the side of his bed, and Matron watched him anxiously. "I think you'd better stay home today. I'll tell Mr. Lehman . . ." She didn't have a chance to finish her sentence, for suddenly Ethan threw himself into her lap and burst into tears. Matron smoothed his hair and patted his back until his sobs ended.

"Now," she said, "suppose you tell me all about it. What is so bad that it's made you sick? You didn't have trouble at school, did you?"

Ethan shook his head. "I don't want to be sent away from here," he gulped.

"Now, why would you worry about that? Nobody is going to send you away."

Suddenly it was impossible to keep it to himself any longer, and Ethan told Matron the whole story, beginning with finding Riley's picture on the floor and seeing Hugh in the bedroom, and ending with all that had happened the day before. Matron listened without interrupting, then hugged Ethan tightly.

"You should have told Mr. Lehman or me all of this at

once," she said, "but I know you were afraid. You've had a lot to worry you since you've been here. Come, we'll talk to Mr. Lehman now. I'll go with you."

Ethan took the box from his cupboard, and Matron tucked it under her arm. She took Ethan's hand in hers, and together they walked down to the office.

Mr. Lehman was not alone. Mr. Quincy was there, and the two men looked very serious.

"We had no idea he would leave before daybreak," Mr. Quincy was saying. "He seemed like a nice young boy. Gridley thought he had real possibilities."

Matron knocked softly on the open door, and Mr. Lehman stood up.

"Come in, Matron. Is something wrong? Is Ethan sick?"

"No, I don't think so. But he has something to tell you." She placed the metal box on the desk in front of the two men.

"Why, where did this come from? Ethan, you didn't . . ."

"No, Mr. Lehman," Matron interrupted him. "He didn't take it. You'd better hear the whole story."

Ethan was more frightened than he had ever been in his life, but he managed to tell the director and Mr. Quincy all that he had told Matron earlier. When he had finished, Mr. Lehman questioned him.

"Have you seen Hugh since he asked you to get the box?"

"No, sir," Ethan replied. "We went fishing, and he was gone when we got back."

"On the morning you saw Hugh in the bedroom, did he take anything?"

"I didn't see him take anything. He just opened and shut the cupboards."

"All right, Ethan. I'm glad you've told us this and brought the money back. You may go on to school now. Matron will write a note to the teacher so you won't be marked tardy."

After they had left, Mr. Quincy spoke.

"We don't have all the pieces of the puzzle yet. If Hugh didn't take the money, who did? And if he did take it, why was it found out by the barn? Had the boy been here long?"

"He came as an infant," Mr. Lehman replied. "He was brought in by a mission worker who had no idea who his parents were. We've never had any request for information about him." Mr. Lehman thought for a moment, then continued. "Until a couple of years ago, he was a happy, cheerful boy. He was disappointed when others were adopted and he wasn't, but there were always boys his age to play with, and Hugh seemed to accept the situation."

"What happened then?" Mr. Quincy inquired.

"When he was about twelve, his special friend, Paul, was taken by a couple who lived several hundred miles from here. Hugh began to change after that. He wasn't openly defiant, but he started to tease the younger children, and, I'm sorry to say, bullied them into doing what he wanted them to do. I don't believe he ever actually stole anything, but he would hide things and suggest that someone else might have taken them. The older fellows, like Riley and Philip, were onto his tricks, but the younger boys were afraid of him."

Mr. Lehman leaned back in his chair and sighed.

"I've talked with him many times about his behavior, and he always promised to do better. But this is the first time he's ever run away. This will be his last year of school, and Hugh is a bright boy. He could have apprenticed in almost any trade he chose if he didn't want to continue his studies."

Mr. Quincy listened quietly to the story. "I think we should find the boy," he said. "I'd like to see him make something of himself."

A sound in the hallway caused both men to look toward the door. There, with his knapsack in his hand and looking very tired, stood Hugh.

15

HUGH MAKES
IT RIGHT

Patterson Quincy sat on the broad porch of his home that evening and looked out over the lawn and garden. The evening paper was on the table beside him, and several matters that he'd not had time to attend to during the day awaited his attention, but his thoughts were not directed toward any of those things. His mind continued to return to the scene in the office of the Briarlane Children's Home that morning.

Although he had been president of the Board of Trustees there for a number of years, Mr. Quincy had not taken a personal interest in anything other than the business affairs of the institution. He had faithfully watched over the legal matters of the home and carefully monitored the details of the running of an orphanage. The fact that the children living there were individuals with different needs and personalities had largely escaped his notice until today.

His mind returned to the scene of this morning. He had observed two badly frightened boys awaiting judgment. That was not an unusual experience for Patterson. He faced the guilty and the innocent daily in his courtroom, and impartially dispensed justice to the best of his ability. Why, then, could he not regard these young boys as just two more in a long line of defendants? As he listened to Hugh Kelly, Patterson Quincy understood the feelings of rejection the boy expressed, and the attempts to take control of a situation that was not of his own making.

While Patterson had not been a homeless child, he had been raised by a couple who had cared for his needs, expected him to plow a few acres of land for the rest of his life, as they had done, and didn't encourage any ideas of "bettering" himself. But Patterson had seen more, and had fought for it.

And so had Hugh, he thought, as he heard the boy's story.

"When Ethan wouldn't get the money for me," Hugh said, "I thought I'd have to make one of the older boys do it. But Matron didn't lock the office door, so I took it myself. I was going to go as far away as I possibly could, and maybe get a job working in a bank."

"But you didn't take the money with you. Why not?" Mr. Lehman asked him.

"I got to thinking that the folks here have been awful good to me. And I'm strong. I can earn my own money. So I brought it back and left it by the barn where Otis would find it."

"Why did you decide to come back today, Hugh? You could have gone on and gotten a job."

"I heard Mr. Quincy talking to you last night," Hugh replied. "I knew you hadn't found the box. Mr. Gridley trusted me with his money, and that felt good. So I decided to come back and take my punishment. I want you to trust me."

The boy was frightened, and Patterson's heart had gone out to him. Hugh was a fighter, and he needed someone to back him up.

All the rest of the day Patterson's thoughts had returned to young Hugh Kelly. He was no longer a name on the roster of the orphanage, but a boy who deserved to have someone take an interest in him and make a difference. Patterson Quincy was that someone.

To his astonishment, Patterson found himself thinking that he would like to adopt Hugh. Unlike Eugenia, who now seemed satisfied to remain childless, Patterson wished for a son to carry on his name, and perhaps even follow in his footsteps. Now here was a boy who had many of the same ambitions Patterson had had as he grew up. This was a boy he'd like to take into his family.

But how would Eugenia feel about it? If there were the least reluctance on her part, Patterson decided, he would abandon the plan immediately. Her happiness was more important to him.

"Eugenia," he began, "I must tell you what occurred today."

Patterson repeated the story, then concluded, "I've been

thinking that I would like to apprentice Hugh. I would encourage him to finish school, then help him get training in the profession he chooses to follow. I'm sure George Lehman would arrange for him to stay at Briars until he could manage on his own. What do you think?"

Eugenia was silent for so long Patterson decided that she must wish to have nothing to do with the idea. Finally she spoke.

"I wouldn't want the boy to remain at the orphanage, Patterson. We have more than enough room here. You'll want to watch his progress, and it seems to me he would benefit from your experience. A child needs a home and a family, don't you think?"

Eugenia returned to her hand work, adding, "Perhaps you would want to give him our name, if that pleases you. There is something very sad about a boy who reaches the age of fifteen without a name that attaches him to somebody. I think your plan is an excellent one."

When the children returned from school in the afternoon, it didn't take long for the news to spread that Hugh had come home.

"He can do whatever he wants to me," Ethan told Bert. "As long as he leaves Alice and the boys alone. Riley'll be glad to have him back. Matron will, too."

Bert nodded. "What'll you do when he finds out you told Mr. Lehman about him?"

"I don't know. You're the only one who knows that,

besides Matron. I had to tell them something, when I came home with all that money. Do you think I should have said I didn't know anything about it?"

Bert considered this. "Naw. It's always best to tell the truth. That way you don't have to keep making up stuff to go with it. But I don't know if Hugh's going to think so."

Ethan was sitting on the back steps when Hugh came out the door.

"Move over, kid," he said. Ethan moved, and Hugh sat down beside him.

"I hear you had a ride in Mr. Quincy's big car."

Ethan nodded.

"Mr. Gridley told me. I rode with him out to the lake. Some car, eh?"

Ethan nodded again. He couldn't think of anything to say, since he had no idea where the conversation was going. He waited for Hugh to continue.

"Say, listen, kid. Mr. Lehman said he asked you if you ever saw me take anything, and you said you didn't. How come you never told him I took the box out of his drawer?"

"I didn't know that," Ethan replied. "I just knew that it was gone and you were gone."

"I took it," Hugh said. "But I never went away with it. I left it out by the barn."

"Yeah. Alice found it there. I had to take it back to Mr. Lehman."

Hugh nodded. "I know. It wasn't your fault. Look. I was mean to you because I was scared you'd talk. I wasn't really going to tell on you."

"I know," Ethan said. "Bert told me they don't do that here. But I didn't know that, and I was scared too. I was afraid Mr. Lehman would send me away."

"He wouldn't do that. The only reason you leave here is if you get adopted. I'm too old for that now, but you might have a chance someday. You're a pretty good kid."

Ethan was pleased. This was the same as Hugh saying that he was sorry. Ethan was willing to forget the past and be friends.

"You going back to school, Hugh?"

"Yeah—think I will. Gridley says Mr. Quincy might give me a job if I work hard. I got to start taking care of myself pretty soon." Hugh stood up and gave Ethan a friendly poke on the shoulder. "See you later, kid."

He sauntered off toward the barn, leaving Ethan to think that his world had turned upright again. Simon and Will were safe during the day, and Alice was in school with him. He had nothing to worry about.

Even so, Ethan's heart skipped a beat when Matron told him after supper that Mr. Lehman wanted to see him in his office.

"You don't have to be scared if you didn't do nothing wrong," Bert assured him. "He prob'ly just wants to tell you something."

Mr. Lehman smiled at Ethan when he entered the office. "I have heard from your older brother, and he sent you a letter," he said.

"From Russell? Does he want us to come home?"

"I'm afraid it's not that," Mr. Lehman replied. "I'm sure

he'll tell you in here." He handed an envelope to Ethan.

"Thank you. Can I read it now?"

"Certainly. Sit there on the sofa if you like."

Ethan turned the letter over in his hand several times before he opened it and pulled out a single sheet of paper.

> *Dear Ethan,*
>
> *I hope you and the others are well. I am writing to tell you that Pa has decided not to come back from the Merchant Marines. He says we can do whatever we want about staying here. Rachel is going to marry John Higgins, and Walter and Jake and I are working on farms. Mrs. Kelly is going to keep Molly, so we're leaving this house.*
>
> *I wrote to Mr. Lehman and told him that you could be adopted now. You'll have a nice family to live with and maybe get to finish school. Don't forget that all of you have to stay together. Ma wanted it that way. Rachel and the others send their love.*
>
> *Your brother,*
Russell

Ethan put the letter down and saw that Mr. Lehman was watching him. "They don't want us anymore."

Mr. Lehman came around the desk and sat down beside Ethan on the sofa. He put his arm around the boy.

"I'm sure they would take you if they could, Ethan," he said. "They have no home together now. It was good of Russell to make arrangements for your future care. I believe he's done the best he could do. I think he's right that some good family may want you."

"All of us," Ethan reminded him. "We all have to go with the same family."

Mr. Lehman agreed. "We'll be sure of that," he said. "You won't be separated."

Matron comforted Ethan when they prayed at bedtime. "Don't forget that the Good Shepherd is watching over all of you," she said. "He'll never allow you to go anyplace that He doesn't go with you. You're His child, Ethan, and He loves you."

Better than my Pa, Ethan thought as he closed his eyes. *At least the Lord keeps His eye on us. I'm glad Matron told me about Him.*

16

AN ADVENTURE
BEGINS

Ethan enjoyed school. "I might even be a teacher so that I can go to school for the rest of my life," he confided to Bert.

"What about being a farmer?" Bert inquired. "You said that's what you would like the best."

"I'll do that too. I can farm before school and after school and on Saturdays."

Bert wasn't sure this was a good idea. It sounded like a lot of work to him. "There's more to farming than hoeing the garden and feeding the animals," he reminded Ethan. "Are you going to stay here at the Briars the rest of your life too?"

Ethan looked at the big orphanage, the barn, and the fields surrounding them. "I wouldn't mind. Since we don't have anyplace to go back to, this is home. I have a lot of years until Will grows up anyway. I can't do anything else until then."

Toward the end of winter, Bert spotted a visitor who was a stranger to the Briars. This was an unusual occurrence, and Bert was quick to report it to Ethan.

"Did you see the man who came to see Mr. Lehman?" Bert said. "He came from the city."

"How can you tell?" Ethan demanded. "He might have come right from Briarlane."

"Nope. I've seen all the people in this town who dress up fancy like that, and he's not one of them. Besides, I heard him ask Otis who the director was here and how to find him. Everyone from town would already know that."

The boys looked toward the house again from their perch on the front fence. "He's staying in there an awful long time," Ethan noted. "I wonder if he'll take someone away with him."

"Not likely. Fathers and mothers come together to choose a kid. This is something else."

When the stranger stayed for dinner, the matter took on a new seriousness. The dining room was quiet, and everyone was on his best behavior as they waited to find out what the visit might mean.

Mr. Lehman looked around and smiled. "These are not the ordinary sounds of mealtime here," he assured the man. "We so seldom have a guest that the children aren't sure what they ought to do. But this does give you the best chance to see them all together."

"This is a nice group of children," the visitor said. "You will have difficulty deciding which ones will benefit most from our program. We will begin to advertise in local newspapers at once for the group who will leave in the spring. I suggest that you have your list ready by the end of April."

Mr. Lehman nodded. "I will have twelve names for you by that time. There will probably be four or five girls in that number. We always have more boys, it seems."

The visitor looked around with approval at the strong, healthy-looking children. "We will have no difficulty placing your children, I'm sure. It might be well to mention this plan in your next letter to your supporters. Some may come forward with a request."

Mr. Lehman thought for a moment. "Several years ago we placed a sister and little brother with a couple who live in the west," he said. "They may be willing to take another child. Our letter goes to many churches out there, so the word will spread quickly."

The visitor was pleased to hear this. "One of our agents and a nurse of your choice will travel with the children. The agent is your link between the Briars and the family who takes a child. He will check the references in each town and act on your behalf. If there are brothers and sisters in your group, we do all we can to place them in the same or nearby communities."

"I have a family of four, ages three to nine," Mr. Lehman told him. "They must go to the same home."

"The same home!" the man exclaimed. "I can't recall anyone ever taking four children at once. Are you sure they can't just be settled close to each other?"

Mr. Lehman shook his head. "It is the expressed wish of

the family, and I have agreed to abide by it. There is very little say that these children have over their lives, and I feel that I must honor my commitment."

"I understand," the man replied. "It would certainly help if we had a request for that many, but we will do our best."

"I believe the Lord will provide a home for the Coopers," Mr. Lehman said. "If this is His purpose for them, it will surely be done."

The visitor agreed, and after discussing other matters concerning the program, he left.

That week Mr. Lehman sent out a letter to friends and supporters of the home explaining the plan to be carried out.

> . . . *Twelve children from the Briarlane Christian Children's Home will be chosen to travel to the western states on the Orphan Train. In each community where the train stops, people will be asked to take a child into their home and raise him as a member of their family. The child will receive an adequate education, religious training, board and room, and the care and consideration a natural child would expect from his parents. I would urge each of you to consider the possibility of welcoming one of these children into your home.*
>
> *Included in Briarlane's twelve will be a family of four children, three boys and a girl. This is the largest number from one family to be offered for adoption in the history of the Home. Since they must be kept together, I am asking that you help us by making inquiry in your church and among your neighbors about*

a family willing to accept these children.
  Please watch your local newspaper for the dates
that the Orphan Train will arrive in your community.

Very shortly after this announcement was sent, the
children at the home were told of the event that would
occur in the spring. There was great excitement as they
listened to Mr. Lehman explain the plan. Most of them had
seen the train that came through Briarlane on the trip
between New York and Chicago, but no one had ever
ridden on one.

"You mean we get to ride to Chicago and someone will
take us home with them?" Philip asked.

"That's right," Mr. Lehman assured him. "But you will
have to go past Chicago. Another train will take you
farther west."

He held up a large map of the United States. "The
Orphan Train will go through Missouri, Iowa, Nebraska,
and Kansas."

There was silence as the boys and girls took this in. It
was hard to believe that such a thing could be possible.

"How many of us gets to go, Mr. Lehman?"

"Twelve of you will leave when school is out," he
replied. "More will be ready to go at the end of the
summer."

Bert looked troubled. "What if our folks come for us
after we're gone?"

"If that should happen, I will know exactly where you
are and will let you know at once. No one will be sent on

the train from Briarlane unless he really wants to go," Mr. Lehman assured them.

Riley was excited about the trip. "I never thought I'd get adopted, being I'm so old," he said. "Are you sure they want big fellows like me?"

"Perfectly sure, Riley. You will be apprenticed, and when you are seventeen you may stay there and earn wages, or you may go out on your own, just as you would if you remained here. The nice thing will be a family of your own."

"Maybe we won't like our family," someone ventured.

"Then you will not have to stay," Mr. Lehman said. "I won't leave you in a home where you are unhappy. You'll be given another place or you may come back here."

The children couldn't imagine not being happy in a real home with real parents, but some of them did have fears about leaving Briarlane.

"What will we do without Matron?" Betsy asked.

"Matron will be traveling with you," Mr. Lehman told her. "She will stay with you until you are in your new home. Then you will have a mama and papa to look after you. Not all orphans are fortunate enough to have a new life offered to them. Some of you have waited a long time to be adopted, and I'm happy to see you get this chance."

As they talked this over among themselves, most everyone agreed that it would be a great adventure. The little ones who were not yet in school knew that something unusual was going to happen, but they weren't old enough to remember what a family was like, if they had ever been a part of one. The older boys and girls looked forward to having the things that they only dreamed about—a mother and father, possibly even brothers and sisters of their own.

Not everyone was anxious to go. When Ethan spoke to Hugh about it, the older boy expressed his view.

"If I have a chance to work for Mr. Quincy, I'd rather stay here." Hugh looked out across the field thoughtfully. "Mr. Quincy likes me, you know. There aren't a whole lot of folks who do. He thinks I can make something of myself, and when I do, I want to be here, where he can see it. How about you? Does it sound like a good idea to you?"

Ethan poked in the dirt with a stick and nodded his head. "I'd like it. But I think Bert is right. Nobody's going to choose a boy who has so much to take care of. And I won't go without them," he said fiercely. "The boys are still little and Alice is a girl. Ma wanted me to be in charge."

Hugh had no answer to that.

As March ended and the time came closer for final arrangements to be made, George Lehman was also concerned over the fate of the Cooper children. This would be a wonderful opportunity for them, but he dared not send them out unless a definite offer had been made to care for them.

"I would rather that all our children had assigned homes," he told his wife. "I'd like to check each family personally before they take a child. I know that isn't possible of course, but I'd feel better about it."

"Yes, so would I. I keep thinking how some will feel if their friends are chosen and they are left to go on to the next town."

Mr. Lehman agreed. "It's not a perfect plan, but I don't feel that I should deprive any child of a chance for a home and a good future. We must do the best we can and trust God to look after their welfare. This may well be the only opportunity some of them have."

The time finally came when the director was forced to make a decision about the twelve who would be sent out. Reluctantly, he made plans to choose four other children for this trip and hoped that the Coopers might be included in the summer group.

"We have to pray about this," Bert said to his friend. "Matron says that the Bible tells us not to worry about things, but to pray and let the Lord know what we want. Have you been doing that?"

Ethan assured him that he had. "I'm not going to worry until school is out and it's time to go," he said. "Then I might worry a little."

But the second week of April a letter arrived that cheered Mr. Lehman and caused great rejoicing among the boys.

Willow Creek, Nebraska
10 April '08

   Dear Sir:

   You may recall that my wife and I adopted two children from your home five years ago. My wife has been longing for a brother or a sister to replace the boy

we lost last year. We read your announcement of the
family of four children available for placement. Our
daughter has begged us to contact you about taking them
into our home. I would prefer to have only the two
youngest, but Frances insists that we must take them all.
We decided that if we are not too late in speaking for
them, that we would be obliged if you would
send them to us on the Orphan Train.
We await your decision in this matter.

Your servant,
C. S. Bush

"There is no reason to worry about this home," Mr.
Lehman said happily. "I understand that Mr. Bush is a good
churchman and is prospering in his land. This is surely an
answer to prayer!"

Bert and Ethan didn't doubt that for an instant. With
great excitement they made preparations to leave Briarlane.
Each child was allowed one small bag for his belongings.
One set of clothes, in addition to what the child wore, was
included.

"You will stay in Chicago for a few days until the train is
ready to finish the trip west," Mr. Lehman told the
children. "The good people at Hull House have made
arrangements for you."

On the day of departure the little group waited to board
the train for the first part of their trip. All of them were a
little frightened, but Riley, the acknowledged leader, spoke
bravely.

"You all know how to act," he said. "I don't want

anyone to disgrace Matron, or he'll answer to me."

Final good-byes were said, and the chosen twelve climbed the steps to the big railcar. Looking out the window, Ethan saw a proud and smiling Hugh standing between his new parents, Patterson and Eugenia Quincy. In his first good suit, Hugh looked handsome indeed.

The train began to move, and Ethan waved to the dear friends that he had made over the past year. He looked at Will, sitting contentedly beside him, and Simon and Alice on the seat facing, and he thought about all that had happened since the trolley ride that had brought them to the Briars in the rain.

What adventures would this new life bring? Ethan didn't know, but he knew that the Good Shepherd would be with them, and he was content.

Other books by Arleta Richardson

In Grandma's Attic
More Stories from Grandma's Attic
Still More Stories from Grandma's Attic
Treasures from Grandma
Sixteen and Away from Home
Eighteen and On Her Own
Nineteen and Wedding Bells Ahead
At Home in North Branch
New Faces, New Friends
Stories from the Growing Years
Christmas Stories from Grandma's Attic
The Grandma's Attic Storybook
The Grandma's Attic Cookbook

The Orphans' Journey Book One: Looking for Home
The Orphans' Journey Book Two: Whistle-stop West

DISCARDED